JAY BENNETT

THE Executioner

AN AVON  FLARE BOOK

Some word changes have been made by the author for this edition.

AVON BOOKS, INC.
1350 Avenue of the Americas
New York, New York 10019

For
DOROTHY *and* SENECA FURMAN
with love

I am the executioner. When the crime is committed and the Lord God does not take vengeance nor does the exalted State move to declare and then to punish, I say when these bitter events happen, then comes the time for the executioner to declare himself or herself as the case may be. I have waited long enough.

So the time has come and I declare myself the executioner.

The three criminals are hereby sentenced to death.

By fire. By water. By earth.

24th day of July 1980

Discovered in vault box No. 1480 of the Cordell Savings Bank, Cordell, New York

1

He stood looking in the mirror at his new face, his eyes dark and somber. He decided he'd take a walk, the first walk since the crackup. He went to the corner of the room and picked up his cane and turned and went to the doorway, out and down the carpeted steps.

Slowly, silently.

When he came downstairs he paused at the opening to the living room. His father got up from the easy chair, put down the newspaper quickly.

"Going out, Bruce?"

"Just for a walk."

"I'll go with you."

Bruce shook his head.

"I'd rather be alone," he said quietly.

His father looked to his mother, a quick look.

"Sure, Bruce. Whatever you want."

"Will you be out long?" his mother asked in her gentle voice.

He sensed the hint of fear that he had brought into the room. He saw the slight tremor in one of his mother's long, slender hands.

"Will you?" she asked again.

9

The tight, awkward way his father bent his head toward him, the light glinting off his glasses.

"I don't know," he said. "Just want to be alone.

"Of course, Bruce."

"Of course," his father echoed.

Bruce turned away from them and went out of the house, down the wooden steps, and into the gathering twilight.

He felt the eyes of his parents at the windows of the house, gazing out after him. His father standing at one window, his mother at the other.

Standing motionless in the slowly fading light.

He heard a neighbor's dog bark, a deep and solemn sound, and then the sound died abruptly and all was still again. The air was quiet and soft. He walked along the tree-shaded street, using the cane to favor his right leg. The leaves overhead lay flat and thick along twisted black branches. The air was quiet and soft and the words of the orthopedist came floating back to him.

You'll soon throw away that cane, Bruce, and you'll be competing in track meets. Just as before. You start your last term of high school in the fall, don't you? Fine. You'll win some gold medals again.

You'll see.

He turned down the lane that led to the water, his shadow getting longer. He came to a row of benches that stretched along a stone esplanade. He sat down on one of the benches and looked out over the reach of the Sound. At the cluster of white boats at a dock. The tinge of pink on the water, the dying summer sun, and out, far out, against a darkening horizon, some sails.

Stark, white, and silent.

He put his hand to his face and slowly drew it away.

As handsome as ever, Bruce. I must say I'm proud of myself.

That's what the plastic surgeon had said.

10

No deep unsightly scars.

The hand went back to the face and this time the fingers slowly traced along the lips, the nose, the eyebrows, then down the chin. And it was like his old face. Very like it.

But something was wrong.

The fingers went back to the eyes and lingered there. Lingered about the dark eyes that had been gazing long into the narrow mirror in his room. And he knew that something strange had come into the new face.

Strange and corrosive.

"The eyes," he whispered. "In the eyes. It's there."

Was it a look of anguish?

Of guilt?

Guilt that would always remain there, never to leave?

"Guilt," he whispered.

The sound of his voice rustled away into the stillness. His hand left his face and fell to his side. Slowly, futilely. It was then that the tears came. The first tears since the crackup.

"I'm a murderer," he said, in a low, bitter voice.

And as he did, he turned around to see who had heard him. But there was no one about. He was alone

Completely alone.

2

He sat there, his hand gripping the cane, the darkness sweeping in over the water and surging onto him, till he was enveloped. And he saw the snow again, the white, falling snow and he drifted back along the swirling current and soon he found himself caught in that cruel night, caught tight and hard and there was no escape.

No escape from that fatal night of the party.

"Christ," he said to himself. "Let me alone. Please let me alone."

But he was caught.

He saw Raymond, tall and lean, get up from a sofa and come over to him.

"I think we ought to beat it."

"Why, Ray?"

"There's nothing doing here. And we don't know anybody."

"So what? We'll get to know them."

"We're out of our territory. Let's go on home."

"I like it here."

"You don't. You're just being stubborn and stupid."

"So I'm stubborn and stupid."

Raymond looked at him and without smiling he

13

reached over and gently brushed back Bruce's damp hair with his lean hand.

"The truth is you've been drinking too much, Bruce. Let's get out of here."

"You've been drinking, too. Everybody's been drinking. It's going to be a great party once it really gets started."

"I've stopped an hour ago. I'm okay. I have to drive."

Bruce shook his head.

"It's too early to leave. This is Saturday night. Crime to leave a party early on a Saturday night. A crime."

"It's almost midnight. Come on, Bruce."

But Bruce still sat in his chair.

"It's still snowing," he said.

"Stopped an hour ago."

"Just like your drinking."

"Uh-huh."

"You got all the answers."

Raymond stood there, not saying anything. Bruce finished his drink and put the glass down.

"All the answers. Just like you do in school. Top man on the totem pole. Man most likely to succeed. Right, Raymond? Right."

Raymond shrugged, without smiling.

"You coming?" he finally said. "Or am I going to leave you here?"

"Now you're threatening me and we grew up together. In Cordell. Dear old Cordell. Just eighteen miles away from here. Or is it nineteen? Or twenty-two? Or what the hell is it, anyway?" His voice trailed off as he said, "Who cares, anyway?"

"It's twenty-four exactly," Raymond said.

"Exactly. Thanks, old buddy. Thanks."

Bruce grinned and gazed up at Raymond's long,

serious face, at the deep brown eyes and the shock of raven-black hair. The thought came to him that Raymond at eighty would look exactly the same as he did at the age of eighteen.

Just a few wrinkles and thin white hair but the same, the same, the same . . .

And act the same. And talk the same.

The same, the same, the same . . .

Raymond's face blurred for an instant and then became clear, blurred and became clear and suddenly Bruce began to laugh.

"All right, preacher," he said. "Let's go. I'm not having fun anyway."

And when they sat in the car, Raymond at the wheel, his floppy hat tight on his head and Bruce lounging beside him, his legs stretched out, the thought came to Bruce that Raymond would live forever.

That type always did.

Forever.

Life was always on their side.

"Life's on your side, Raymond," he laughed. "On your side."

"What's so funny now?" Raymond asked, not turning his head from the snowy road.

"On your side, not on my side," Bruce laughed and then began singing the words over and over again.

Till Raymond cut in sharply, "Okay, so it's on my side. Will you let me drive in peace? Will you, Bruce?"

Bruce slowly stopped laughing.

"Just a funny thought," he grinned.

"You're drunk."

"No. Just happy. Want me to drive?"

"Hell, no."

"I know this road like my own hand."

"Great. Just sit there."

"Let me wear your hat, Ray."

And he reached over for the hat. Raymond jerked his head away and the car swerved.

"Will you cut it out, Bruce? You want to rack us up?"

But Bruce laughed.

"I like your hat. Always liked your hat. It doesn't belong on your head. It goes against your whole life-style. It's a crazy hat and you're a preacher type."

Raymond drove silently, his lips pressed together.

"Well, Ray?"

"Well, what?"

"You goin' to let me wear the hat for a little while? Just a little while?"

"Why?"

"It'll help sober me up."

"What?"

"It will, Ray."

Raymond's hands gripped the wheel and then slowly relaxed. When he spoke, his voice was low and hard.

"Three drinks and it knocks you off. You ought to cut down. Or stop the damn hard stuff altogether. Stick to a few beers and let it go at that."

"Beers?"

"Yes."

"Why beers?"

"I told you why."

"You didn't. Everybody drinks hard stuff, don't they? Gin, whiskey, Scotch. Don't they? Well?"

Raymond drove on without answering.

"Well, don't they? My father drinks and I've seen him crocked. And your father drinks and he's chief of police of Cordell. Right? Right."

"I've never seen my father crocked."

"C'mon. Sure you have."

"Lay off, Bruce. Will you?"

16

Bruce laughed.

"Don't get so serious, Ray. The whole world drinks these days. The President of the United States. The Secretary General of the United Nations. Baseball players. Football players. Soccer players. Chess players. The cats. Kids in school and kids in college. The dogs. Housewives and business executives. It's a drinking world. You want to know why?"

"Why?"

Bruce touched Raymond gently on the shoulder. It was a gentle, warm touch. Raymond glanced over to him and he saw the sad and fearful look that had abruptly settled onto Bruce's face. For a moment he thought that Bruce was going to break down and cry.

"Because it's a desperate world," Bruce said. "That's what it is. A desperate world. I've got a theory on that. Want to hear it?"

"No."

"Goin' to tell you anyway. It's a desperate world because everybody is afraid that it's all going to go up in one big explosion. One big bang and it's all over. For good. For keeps. No more tomorrows and no more yesterdays. No more of anything. Got it?"

"Yes," Raymond said.

"And everybody is scared. Underneath it all they're scared. And there's nothing they can do about it. Nothing."

"There are people who are doing something. Peace groups. Environmental groups. All sorts of thinking and feeling people who . . ."

"Sure, sure," Bruce cut in. "And they get nowhere."

"Maybe if you and other guys got in with them they would get somewhere. Maybe you'd stop getting crocked every Saturday night. Maybe you'd get a little hope and sense and some direction into your life."

"Preacher. Preacher."

17

"It's the truth, Bruce."

"You get crocked, too. Only you hold it better. That's what. You hold it better."

Raymond looked away from him and they drove on in silence.

"Give me the hat, Ray." Bruce suddenly said. "Give it to me, old buddy."

"Still with the hat.'

"It'll sober me up."

"I know."

Raymond took the hat off with his right hand and dropped it onto Bruce's lap.

"Wear it and leave me alone."

"You're my best friend. I ever tell you that?"

"Wear it and shut up."

Bruce delicately put the hat on his head, tilted it to a rakish angle, and laughed. It was a gray felt hat with a large, floppy brim and on its front panel was the USC insignia.

The gold threading of the insignia glinted in the darkness.

"I love this hat," Bruce said. "First time I saw it on you I wanted it."

Raymond's brother Oliver had bought the hat at the University of Southern California's general store. He had promised to get Bruce one when he returned to the Coast in the fall for his sophomore year.

"I like Oliver," Bruce murmured.

"You were quiet for five minutes. I thought you were sleeping your jag off."

"I like Oliver," Bruce said again.

"Good."

"He's a helluva guy. Just the opposite of you."

"He is."

"He's a fun guy."

"And I'm a preacher."

"You got it. Right on the nose."

"And I'm going to live forever."

A car sped by them, its headlights glowing and then the night closed in upon them again.

"Forever and a day," Bruce said.

"Thanks, old buddy."

"You're welcome, old buddy," Bruce murmured, his eyes getting heavy again.

He slouched down in his seat and closed his eyes.

For a long while the two did not speak to each other. As if somehow during this interval of slow, inevitable time they seemed to sense the fate that lay ahead of them that night.

Sensed it deep within them.

On the sides of the winding road, the snow stretched white over the flat fields, white and still.

There was no moon.

"You're right. It was no fun without Marian," Bruce murmured.

Raymond glanced over to him and smiled.

"You miss her."

Marian Clark and Janet Stoner had gone into New York with their parents to see a play and then stay over the weekend.

Bruce opened his eyes.

"Getting used to her."

"Uh-huh."

"And Janet?" Bruce asked.

"She's okay."

"Just okay?"

"I like her."

"That's better."

"Yes," Raymond finally said. "I like her a lot."

And Bruce thought that sooner or later, after Raymond graduated and went out to USC and then went on to become an architect like Oliver planned to do, maybe then or sometime along the way, Raymond and Janet would get married.

Raymond Warner and Janet Stoner.

"Er and er," Bruce said.

"What?"

"Warner and Stoner end in er and er. The two ers unite."

And it suddenly started him laughing again.

"So what?"

"I don't know. Just thought about Janet and you and started laughing."

"Why?"

"Er and er."

"What's so funny about me and Janet?"

"I don't know. Everything's funny to me tonight."

"So I've noticed."

Bruce stopped laughing.

"Funny and desperate," he said. "Like I'm standing on a cliff and swaying. Swaying and about to fall in."

There was something in his voice that made Raymond slow the car down almost to a stop and look over to him.

"How do you feel?"

"All right."

"You're starting to look clammy and white. How's your stomach?"

"Feel all right. I really do."

"That's what you said last time."

"Don't worry. I'll make it home."

"Without throwing up?"

"I told you I'm all right."

"This is Oliver's car. He'll kick like a mule if you mess it up."

"I'll make it home."

"You don't know Oliver like I do."

"I know Oliver."

"He's a fun guy but he doesn't like his car messed up."

"I'm okay."

They drove on and then Raymond spoke.

"I see Carlson's up ahead. Maybe I ought to stop off and get you some black coffee."

"Okay with me, Ray."

"You could use some."

"I guess I could."

"Carlson's big on drinks. You know that."

"Only coffee, Ray. Black, black coffee. I'll only take coffee."

"Remember. Don't give me a hard time."

"I won't. You're my friend. My lifelong buddy. My . . ."

"Okay," Raymond broke in wearily. "Turn it off. Turn it off."

"Turn it off. Turn it on. Off and on." Bruce began to sing the words. "Off and on. On and off . . .

Off and on.

On and off.

Sitting in the darkness, the cane at his side, Bruce remembered again the red neon sign flashing on and off in the night, on and off, CARLSON'S and then blackness, CARLSON'S and blackness, on and off, on and off, till the sight became a horrible, unendurable sound, like a bell with a never-ending jangling voice, CARLSON'S, CARLSON'S, CARLSON'S, and he thrust his two hands to his ears and held them tight against the sound.

His breath came in dry gasps.

CARLSON'S.

CARLSON'S.

CARLSON'S.

He rose from the bench and stood rigidly, his face contorted.

21

His new face.

"I don't want to go into Carlson's," he cried aloud. "Take me home, Ray. Take me home."

His voice echoed against the wall of darkness and dropped away.

He stood in silence.

Dead silence.

3

They went into Carlson's and sat down at a table. They were in their home territory. All about them were people they knew.

Ed Millman, who was on the track team with Bruce, and Elaine Ross, Ed's date for the night, came over to join them. They carried steins of beer in their hands.

"Where've you been?"

"A party in Lawrenceville," Raymond said.

"How was it?"

"Dull, dull, dull," Bruce said. "I need a drink. Need one bad."

"I'll get the coffee," Raymond said, getting up. "The joint's hopping. We'll never get any service."

"It's Saturday night," Ed smiled.

"It's Saturday night and a beer will do the trick." Bruce laughed as he grabbed the stein from Ed's hand and began to drink from it.

"Lay off, will you, Bruce?" Raymond said angrily.

"Oh, let him have it," Ed laughed.

"He's crocked. Can't you see it?"

"We're all crocked," Elaine laughed. "Crocked or on our way to being crocked."

23

The four-piece band that played every Saturday night ended a set and segued into a new one.

Bruce grinned as he heard the music.

"I feel good again," he said. "I feel good. Like I'm floating on water with the sun all over it. A great, great feeling."

And Bruce standing in the well of darkness, hand gripping the cane, heard his bubbling words again and remembered sitting in Carlson's, the nausea leaving him and a feeling of wild exhilaration taking over as he drank more beer with Ed and Elaine, and Raymond sitting there, not drinking, just glowering at them.

Raymond finally got them into his car.

Elaine and Ed fell asleep on the back seat, their arms around each other. Bruce sat in the front with Raymond.

"I feel great, Ray. And I'll behave. I really will."

"Swell."

"Drop off Ed and Elaine first and then take me home, old buddy. I feel great."

Raymond glared at him and without a word turned again to the wheel. Bruce lay back against the seat and closed his eyes, a big happy grin on his lips.

And yet even then the thought came to him that it was a strange night. Something deathly wrong with it. Full of weird contradictions. Instead of the glasses of beer making him violently sick at Carlson's, they seemed to set him up better. To settle his stomach and fevered senses.

It was a strange night.

Strange and ominous he suddenly thought, and as he did, a chill flowed through him. His hands trembled.

The wide, happy grin left his lips.

After a long stillness Raymond glanced over to Bruce, a quick, appraising look, and it seemed to him that Bruce had become rigid. He was sitting upright, back straight against the seat. sitting like a stone statue His eyes cold and staring.

And then the eyes closed and in the shadowed light the face became a mask.

They rode along in complete silence. A vast, enveloping stillness. Not even the sound of the wheels was heard.

Not even that.

Then as if on signal, an eerie, chilling signal, Bruce's eyes snapped open and he became aware of the hat on Raymond's head.

The floppy hat.

And just as suddenly the drunken sensation swirled over him.

"The hat, Ray."

"What about it?"

"The hat."

Bruce lurched over for the hat and the car swerved sharply and then Raymond was able to bring it back onto the road again.

"Bruce, will you . . ."

"You took the hat 'way. My hat."

Raymond slowed the car down almost to a halt.

"I'm going to stop this car and dump you now. That's what I'm going to do."

"C'mon, Ray. Settle down. Come on, old buddy "

"Don't give me that 'old buddy' crap."

"You're not goin' to leave me alone in the night. Not that, Ray."

"What's wrong?" Ed asked, his eyes slowly opening.

"This crazy Bruce is trying to rack us up."

"Oh, Bruce is okay," Ed murmured. "He's a happy fella. We're all happy fellas. All of us."

And he kissed Elaine on the forehead and closed his eyes again.

"All of us," Elaine murmured, never opening her eyes.

And later on when the two were questioned, they remembered nothing. Absolutely nothing. It was all a blank.

They remembered getting into the car and falling asleep.

Everybody had been drinking, they said.

Everybody?

Yes.

And that's all they honestly remembered.

The driver, too?

Raymond Warner? Ray?

Well? Was he drunk, too?

Everybody. We were all crocked. All of us.

The swift hours at Carlson's had become a blur to them. A blur of beer steins, of heady music, and of smoky faces.

Yes, they murmured sadly. Ray drank along with us.

Raymond's voice rose against the night.

"Bruce, are you going to lay off? Are you?"

"Don't get angry at me, Ray," Bruce pleaded. "Don't, old buddy. Please don't." His face screwed up and he was about to weep maudlin tears. "I can't take it, Ray. I can't, old buddy."

He raised his arms and moved forward, about to put them around Ray and soothe his anger.

"Move away from me, damn you. Move away."

"Okay, Ray. Okay."

Like a scolded child Bruce moved away from him.

"And stay over there till I get you home."

"I will, Ray. I will."

Bruce nodded his head solemnly again and again and Ray looking at the nodding head didn't know whether to laugh or shout in frustration.

When he spoke his voice was low and controlled.

"Close your eyes and try to sleep it off."

"Sure thing, Ray."

"Close them."

"Okay. Okay."

Bruce dutifully closed his eyes.

"And keep them shut. Your mouth, too."

Soon the silence came down upon them again.

"I was a damn fool," Raymond thought. "A damn fool to stop off at Carlson's."

They were now nearing the outskirts of Cordell. The road lay ahead of them, smooth and glistening. Earlier in the night the snowplows had cleared away most of the snow, throwing up white banks that bordered each side of the road.

It must've happened about three o'clock in the morning. The State Police put it at about three-fifteen or three-twenty. Dan Warner, police chief of Cordell, estimated it at about three twenty-five.

But nobody really knows.

When it happened.

Or why it happened.

The *Cordell Chronicle* for three solid days ran an extended editorial on drunken driving and the irresponsible behavior of the young of the community.

The editorial lashed out at the driver of the car.

Raymond Warner, son of the police chief, Daniel Warner.

Carlson's should be closed down once and for all.

There were more than a hundred letters agreeing with the scathing editorial but the truth is that no one knows what really happened.

That is, no one but Bruce Kendall.

He knows quite well.

And he remembers.

27

All of it.

"All of it," Bruce whispered.

The car sped along piercing the darkness of the waning night. The headlights flashed up the long road like two spears. The trees stood bare and leafless.

Raymond glanced over to Bruce and saw his head tucked into his chest, his eyes closed. He was fast asleep.

Raymond sighed. Bruce is okay, he thought. A pain in the butt sometimes but he's okay. Everybody likes Bruce. The girls especially. He's a handsome guy and a sweet fellow. But he sure gave me a tough time tonight. Well, any minute I'll reach his house and drop him off.

Soon.

And then I'll be able to breathe again.

He put his foot hard on the accelerator and the car jumped forward as if it were a live being. It sped by a lone telephone pole, the shadow of the pole dark and long on the white snow, and it was then, the instant they crossed the black shadow, as if it were a dividing line between life and death, it was then that Bruce opened his eyes and saw the floppy hat on Raymond's head.

The absurd hat on the absurd head.

"The hat," he whispered.

And then his laughter shattered the silence. Raymond shivered as he heard it.

"Keep away, Bruce."

"It's crazy there on top of your skull."

"Bruce."

"Crazy. Crazy."

"Bruce, for the love of Christ . . ."

But Bruce had already reached up and grabbed the

hat from Raymond's head with a violent and jarring motion.

"Bruce!"

The car lurched off the road and with a loud and despairing sound crashed into the huge trunk of an oak tree.

The last thing Bruce heard was Raymond's scream

4

Ed and Elaine were thrown clear of the car and landed in a snowbank. They were unhurt. Bruce had to be pried loose from the front end of the car. He was rushed to a hospital and for many weeks he hovered between life and death. Raymond Warner died instantly.

Bruce sat there on the bench listening to the calm ripple of the water and thought of Raymond.

Heard again the last piercing scream.

"I killed you," he whispered. "It was all my fault, Ray. All mine."

His voice broke and he lifted his hand from the cane and covered his eyes. He tried to drive the memories away but they would give him no peace.

They surged back.

He was lying in the hospital and the door of the room opened, opened quietly, and the nurse came over to him with Oliver Warner at her side.

Raymond's brother Oliver.

"Bruce, I've brought you a visitor."

"Thanks."

She turned to Oliver.

"Just a few minutes. Remember now."

31

"I will."

Then she closed the door and left them alone.

"How do you feel, Bruce?" Oliver asked gently.

Bruce couldn't speak. He just lay there looking up at Oliver. And Bruce thought how like Raymond he is. The same height, the same rangy figure, the same shock of black hair hanging over his forehead . . . and yet he is not the same.

Raymond had been serious and dogged. Oliver is loose and easy. Nothing ever seems to faze him. He can handle anything, Raymond once said. Nothing flaps him. Nothing. And he can drink and be wild and then laugh the whole thing off.

He's really a fun guy.

But now his eyes, he had quiet blue eyes that could light up with an amused gleam, now they were sad and tender.

"I've been here a few times to see you, Bruce. But they wouldn't let me in. No visitors for a long time."

"Just my folks."

Oliver nodded and the sun coming through the open windows glinted off his black hair.

"You've been here quite a while, Bruce. How do you feel?"

"Coming along."

"That's good."

"My body's starting to feel okay again."

"Swell."

"I'm getting a new face. So they tell me."

"Yes," Oliver said softly.

They were silent.

"Oliver," Bruce said, breaking the silence, "I've been waiting for you to come here."

"Been out on the Coast, Bruce. At school."

"And when you were here they wouldn't let you in."

Oliver nodded.

"That's it, Bruce."

"I've been waiting," Bruce said.

They were silent again.

"Oliver."

"Yes?"

"There's something I must tell you."

Oliver looked at him, a gentle, appraising look.

"You're not to talk to much. Nor to upset yourself."

"But . . ."

"Strict orders, Bruce."

"But I must tell you. Only you, Oliver. I've been waiting too long. Keeping it inside of me."

Oliver shook his head and reached over and brushed Bruce's hair gently. Bruce remembered with a sharp ache Raymond doing the same thing to him at the party in Lawrenceville. Raymond brushing his damp hair and saying, You've been drinking too much, Bruce.

"Some other time, Bruce," Oliver said. "When you're stronger."

"I must. Now."

Oliver sighed low.

"About the accident?"

"Yes," Bruce said.

A haunting sadness came into Oliver's eyes.

"I thought so."

"Oliver, I must tell you what happened."

"There's nothing to say."

"But . . ."

"Nothing. He was your best friend. We know how you feel."

And Bruce looking up at Oliver knew what he had known for a long, long time, that if he couldn't tell Oliver the truth then he would never be able to reveal it to anybody else. Not to his father. Not to his mother. Not to Marian.

To no one in this world.

For Oliver standing there was Ray. It was like talking to Ray. Asking him for his forgiveness. If Oliver forgave then some of the guilt would be bearable.

Then Bruce would tell everybody what really happened.

But only then.

He must tell Oliver. He must.

"You've got to hear me out," Bruce said.

"Bruce, let it alone."

But Bruce went on.

"Oliver, the way it really happened was . . ."

Oliver shook his head and his eyes were firm and cold.

"Enough," he cut in. "We know how it happened."

"You do?"

"Yes, Bruce. We know."

Bruce stared at him and didn't speak. Within him a chill had settled.

"My father and I have discussed it many times."

"And?"

"Raymond wasn't much of a drinker. That's all it was."

Bruce stared at him.

"What do you mean that's all it was?"

Oliver sighed and looked away from him

"I drink and hold my stuff. Raymond couldn't."

"So he was drunk that night? Is that it?"

"I'm afraid he was."

"Oliver, this is wrong. You've got it wrong."

Oliver put his hand on Bruce's wrist. His hand was like a manacle, cold to the touch.

"Stop trying to defend him."

"But I'm not."

"Stop it, Bruce. Please."

Bruce looked desperately at him but didn't speak. Oliver let the hand go.

"Forget that night. We're all trying to forget it, Bruce."

"Forget it?"

"I know how hard it is for you. It's hard for all of us. Raymond had a few drinks too many. You all had. And that's how it happened."

"No. That's not how it happened. You've got to hear me out."

Oliver's lips shut tight and grim. When he spoke his voice was harsh.

"It's over, Bruce. Do you hear me?"

"Oliver . . ."

"We don't want it brought up anymore."

You're slamming the door on me, Bruce thought bitterly. How can I let people think that Ray was the guilty one when it was I?

How, Oliver?

"Please listen to me," he said. "Please."

"No, Bruce," Oliver said. "No. You've been through hell. So have we. Thank God my mother is dead so she didn't have to go through this." He paused and then went on, his voice softer. "You have a rough time ahead of you, Bruce. All that plastic surgery coming up yet. No, Bruce. Let's close this affair. Once and for all. Will you promise me that?"

"Please, Ray," Bruce said.

"Ray?"

Bruce turned his head away and was silent. Then he heard Oliver's voice again.

"Promise me, Bruce."

There was a tree with spring blossoms on it and Bruce lay there watching it. He saw a bird flutter down on one of the gleaming branches.

Christ, why can't it always be spring? he thought. Why do we have to have winter and snow?

Why must there be night and roads and snow?

35

Then he heard himself murmur, "All right, Oliver. If that's the way you and your father want it. You and your father."

"That's the way we want it."

Bruce blotted out the sun and the glittering sky and the white spring blossoms and looked again into Oliver's set face.

"All right," he said.

Oliver's face softened and the haunting sadness came back into the blue eyes.

"It's over, Bruce," he said tenderly. "Think of the future. Forget the past."

"Forget the past," Bruce said mechanically.

Oliver patted Bruce's hand affectionately. Like a big brother. Bruce felt again the icy coldness of Oliver's fingers.

"It's over," Oliver said. "Nothing will ever call it back. Nothing will change one single minute of it. It's gone forever, Bruce."

"Yes," Bruce whispered.

"So don't ever bring that subject up again. As a favor to both of us. It's better for you this way, too, Bruce. Much better."

Bruce didn't say anything.

"Don't you think so?"

"Maybe."

"Well?"

"I won't," Bruce said.

"Ever?"

The nurse opened the door and came into the room.

"You must go now," she said briskly.

"I won't ever bring it up again," Bruce said to Oliver. "To you or anybody else in this world."

"Good-bye, Bruce."

"Good-bye, Oliver."

"I'll have to go back to the Coast. I'll see you in the

36

summer. We'll spend some time together and get to know each other better. Now that Ray is gone."

Bruce just lay there looking up at him.

"Okay?"

"Okay, Oliver," Bruce said.

Oliver smiled broadly and waved his hand. Bruce watched the tall figure go out of the room.

"What's wrong, Bruce?" the nurse asked gently.

He turned away from her without answering and lay there staring at the blank wall.

5

The door had been slammed shut. He would never open it again.

Bruce sat on the bench in the dark night and smiled bitterly to himself. What the hell else could I do?

That's the way Oliver and Dan Warner wanted it. I guess that's the way Ray would've wanted it too.

Let it all die and be forgotten.

Would he?

Ah, who knows?

But that's the way they want it.

And so nobody learned the truth. Not a single soul. Over the long, agonizing months he had some brief, groping talks with his father and mother but he never told them the truth of that fatal night. And then as if by silent agreement they pushed away the night and banished it.

Life was easier and tidier that way For all concerned.

Bruce smiled again. Yes, it was.

And he thought of Marian.

Although he felt close to her at times and enjoyed her visits to him in the hospital he never broke his word to Oliver. And she was considerate and tactful enough never to mention the accident

Janet Stoner?

Bruce remembered sitting in the car and singing Stoner and Warner, er and er. The two ers joining together. And Raymond getting angry at him.

Janet Stoner came only once to the hospital to see him. A formal visit. She had always liked Bruce and he had admired her and thought she and Raymond made a swell pair. But now he sensed underneath her polite talk and concern a cold, icy rage at him. Her great hopes and plans had been smashed against the brutal oak tree. Janet Stoner loved Raymond Warner. Young as they were, they loved each other. A lifetime love. Now he could never be her husband and she would never be his wife. She would never share with pride his successful career as an architect. She would never see the buildings he and his brother Oliver would create together. It was all gone, gone forever.

Bruce wondered if somehow she had grasped the truth of that night and knew that he was to blame for Raymond's death. She had small, dark and eloquent eyes that now seemed to pierce through him, even when she was smiling at him. Her voice at times took on a cutting edge. Her laughter was not warm at all, it was slight and brittle. It chilled him. When she finally left the hospital room, Bruce lay back on his bed and slowly closed his eyes. A great weariness came over him. There's one thing I'm sure of, he said to himself. She has come to hate me

With all her being.

He saw again the eloquent eyes as he sat on the bench and gazed into the darkness. They pierced into him and he thought, I deserve to be hated.

The eyes vanished and all he saw was the night and all he heard was the quiet rippling of the water.

"I deserve to die for what I did," he said in a low, broken voice.

The words floated away into the night and suddenly there was a stillness. Cold and pervading. He heard nothing, not even the ripples of the water. He sat there and his lips began to tremble. And it was at that shivering instant that he was sure someone had materialized behind him in the darkness and was standing watching him.

Tall, motionless, and vengeful.

His flesh began to crawl, but he would not turn to the standing figure. He bent forward, fist tight about the handle of his cane, all of his fevered senses alert. Gazing fiercely toward the water. He heard a slight rustling sound. Almost like leaves, dead leaves of an oak tree sweeping along the pavement.

He listened.

Yes, he was sure the sound was that of the leaves of an oak tree. Of a huge oak tree. A tree whose trunk was dark and clotted with blood.

His face blanched and his breath quickened.

The leaves rustled and he listened to it again, like one hypnotized. He waited with a cold dread for the figure that stood shrouded in the darkness to call out to him with a harsh, jangling voice,

Murderer. I'm here to do justice. A life for a life. I'm here to kill you.

He waited but still he would not turn to the silent figure.

Again the rustling of the leaves began and this time he could contain himself no longer. He rose and turned abruptly to the direction of the horrible sound, his eyes large and staring. He desperately sought out the figure of the avenger standing there in the dark. He looked frantically down the rows of benches but he saw no one.

Nothing but the harsh form of the benches.

There was no one standing there.

"No one," he whispered through dry, quivering lips.

He heard again the rustling, the leaves over the pavement, dry and crackling, like winter leaves over a desolate, wintry pavement.

Then the sound gradually faded away.

Nothing.

He stood in a well of black emptiness.

Then slowly, gradually he heard again the faint rippling of the water of the Sound. Rippling and rhythmical.

His hands slowly stopped their trembling. He bent over and slowly picked up the cane where it had fallen from his loosened grasp.

He gripped it and then straightened up.

He breathed in deeply and sighed low. I must watch out, he said to himself. Or I'll fall into the pit. I'll end up hearing and seeing things all the time, night and day, and then they'll come and carry me away to a padded cell and throw the key away. I must watch out and hold. on.

I must hold on.

Oliver is right. Forget the past. Forget it.

I must try to do that. I must.

He stood there listening to the rhythmical sound of the water and it began to soothe him. Far out he saw the light of a boat. It was like a little winking star. He stood there staring at it with a strange fascination, a wild smile in his eyes.

He stood there watching the star till finally the soft summer night blew it out. And now there was nothing but night and sea.

Nobody knows the truth, he said to himself.

Forget the past.

Forget it.

6

It was when he turned into the lane that led away from the water, just as he set the tip of his cane onto the grass that he heard the footsteps on the edge of the cement walk of the esplanade.

And he knew then that there was no forgetting the past.

For the footsteps were cold and measured as they approached the entrance to the lane. He turned and the footsteps stopped abruptly. Bruce peered through the arch of the trees to the opening but he saw nothing.

Just a patch of dark sky.

I heard the footsteps, he said to himself. I'm sure I heard them. It was not my crazy imagination.

Someone is watching me. Someone is really following me.

He turned and started walking through the half light of the silent lane. He heard the footsteps come off the stone and onto the grass.

Now they were soft and gliding.

But he heard them. He knew he heard them.

Bruce stopped walking and swung about and as he did the footsteps stopped. Only the stillness of the night remained.

"Who is it?" he called out.

But there was no answer.

"What do you want of me?"

Again nothing but his voice against the flat stillness. He strained his eyes till he could make out the outlines of a shadow on the grass next to a large elm tree. A shadow that was long and wavering.

He stood there, his cane raised high like a weapon.

"Why are you following me?"

He heard his voice tight and hard fade away into the night. The shadow still lay on the grass, angular and still.

"Damn you, let me alone."

Then the sound of low laughter floated down to him, low and mad. He could not make out whether it was the laughter of a man or a woman.

But the laughter was low and mad and mocking.

And then it stopped.

And only the shadow remained.

Bruce gasped, turned, and began to walk as fast as he could away from the cold, silent shadow. But again he heard the footsteps. Gliding over the grass. They were faster this time. Keeping sure pace with him.

"Let me alone," he muttered in panic. "Let me alone."

He came out of the lane and onto the sidewalk that led to his house. He breathlessly hurried along it moving from pool of lamplight into darkness and then again into the icy, shimmering light.

He looked desperately around for someone to help him. But he was alone. Completely alone under the spaced trees and light and darkness.

The footsteps ever behind him. Now hard and metallic on the stone.

"Please. Please let me alo . . ."

Suddenly he heard them stop. He went a bit farther

and then turned and peered down the block. For an instant he saw no one. And then he saw a dark figure, glinting with lamplight, glide behind the cover of a tree.

Its shadow lay across the walk.

"Bruce."

The voice came from behind him. Bruce turned about wildly and saw the car at the curb just ahead of him. It glistened where the lamplight fell upon it. The rest of the car was in darkness.

"Bruce," the voice called again.

He breathed in deeply and walked slowly over to the car and saw Dan Warner at the wheel.

He was alone.

"Hop in and I'll take you home. Save you a few blocks walk."

The man's impassive face hovered between the lamplight and the gloom. The visor of his police cap had a thin and golden gleam about its edges.

"All right," Bruce murmured.

"You look a bit upset. Anything wrong?"

The man's police eyes gazed calmly up at him.

"No, Mr. Warner," Bruce said. "I'm okay."

He still stood outside the car. But he was now in control of himself. The panic had left him. But there were glistening beads of sweat on his forehead and he saw Warner's eyes fixed upon them.

"You sure?" the man asked quietly.

"Yes."

Bruce glanced away from the scanning eyes and looked down the block. The shadow still lay across the walk, a dark, wavering blot.

"Then hop in."

Bruce opened the door and sat down in the car. He felt safe and warm again.

"Thanks, Mr. Warner," Bruce said and pulled the door shut. The sound was loud and sharp against the still night. He looked again and the shadow slid off the walk and was gone. Only the long vista of a night street remained.

"Something back there bothering you, Bruce?"

"Nothing."

And yet he wondered if Dan Warner knew. Then he pushed away the thought. The car started up and moved away from the curb. They rode along the tree-lined street.

"Saw you walking," Warner said. "And thought I'd give you a lift. How do you feel?"

Bruce shrugged and didn't answer.

"Still using the cane, I see."

"I guess I'll be using it for a long time to come," Bruce said.

"You'll throw it away soon."

Bruce shook his head.

"Maybe I'll never throw it away."

Warner's voice was gentle when he spoke.

"Now don't say that, Bruce. I'll be sitting in the stands, watching you run and win some gold medals like you used to do. I'm sure of that."

"I don't see it ever happening again," Bruce said.

"Why? The doctors tell you that?"

"No."

"Then why?"

"Just feel that way," Bruce said.

The police eyes glanced over to him and appraised him and Bruce thought how like Ray's serious, appraising eyes they are. It's like sitting in the car with Ray again on that night.

Yet the eyes are not Raymond's eyes. There is a hard sadness deep in the man's eyes. Hard and cruel.

Even vengeful.

Why shouldn't there be?

Maybe he already suspects the truth?

"This your first outing, Bruce?"

"Outing?"

"First time you've been out of the house?"

"Yes," Bruce said and wondered how he knew it.

"Had a pleasant walk?"

And again the police eyes scanned him.

"Yes," Bruce said.

"Where did you go?"

"Down to the esplanade."

"Anybody sitting there this time of the night?"

Bruce shook his head.

"No. I saw no one," he said.

Dan Warner grunted and his large hand opened and closed about the rim of the wheel. He was taller than his two sons but unlike them he had a broad and powerful build. His face was lean and lined.

He had gray eyes that could become wintry cold.

"How long did you sit there?"

It's as though I'm in the police station and he's interrogating me, Bruce thought. And yet he's doing it under the guise of a friendly talk.

"A few hours, I guess."

They rode along in silence and then Warner slowed the car down and pulled it over to the curb. They had come to Bruce's house.

"So you've been keeping to yourself, Bruce."

"Yes."

"But now we'll be seeing you about town a bit."

"Maybe."

"I guess we will. You know about Carlson's, don't you?"

Bruce shook his head and then finally spoke.

"Only that I don't expect ever to walk in there again."

Warner looked impassively at him. His big leathery hand opened and then closed again over the wheel.

47

Bruce sensed the pain that was flashing through the man.

"You won't ever walk in there again, Bruce," Warner said in a flat voice. "You or anybody else. The place is shut down. For good."

"What?"

Warner nodded grimly.

"Happened just after the . . . accident." He paused a long while and Bruce could see the jaw clamped shut and the thin line of the lips. "I don't want to go into this, Bruce, but I'm a policeman and I have to tell you. And then we'll drop the subject for good."

Bruce waited.

"The town council just went in and shut the door. Slapped a heavy fine on him. Knocked him on his butt."

So he, too, was smashed up that night, Bruce thought. He, too.

"Carlson's very bitter about all this. The closing came at a bad time for him. He's a ruined man."

"So they shut him down," Bruce murmured.

"He's selling his house and leaving town."

Bruce turned away from him and looked to his own house. The lights were on downstairs and he knew that his parents were inside waiting for him.

He heard Dan Warner's voice.

"I'm telling you all this for a good reason, Bruce. Carlson's a very bitter man. And bitter, ruined people can do unreasonable things."

"They can," Bruce said almost in a whisper.

"He feels he's being made the fall guy. He claims that he came over to your table and tried to stop you from drinking anymore. Tried to get you all to leave but you laughed at him. Do you remember any of that, Bruce?"

"No," Bruce said.

But he remembered every moment of it. Carlson appealing to them to get out and go home. And he, laughing and teasing Carlson. And then Ed and Elaine joining in. Raymond had left the table at the time.

He remembered the man's pale and livid face.

"I don't want to stir up any memories, Bruce. Not for you and not for me. But I feel that I have to."

And Bruce wanted to say to him, I killed your son. Let me tell you how I did it. Let me clear him once and for all. Let me free my conscience so that I can breathe again.

Dan Warner, I killed Raymond.

"I understand," Bruce said.

"He seems to be exceptionally bitter at you, Bruce. Claims that you in particular gave him a hard time that night."

The police eyes were quietly examining Bruce's face. But deep within the same eyes Bruce thought he could see a veil of hatred.

"And that is what Carlson says?" Bruce asked.

"Uh-huh."

"I don't remember the night, Mr. Warner," Bruce said. "I'm doing my best to forget it. Like it never happened."

Warner grunted and then slowly nodded.

"So if you see him on the street in town make sure you cross over to the other side. And then get out of his sight."

"I will," Bruce said.

"I don't want any more trouble here. We've had enough. Enough for a lifetime. Don't you agree?"

"Yes, Mr. Warner," Bruce said.

"Trouble and heartbreak."

"I know." Bruce said in a low voice.

He saw the lights in the lower front of the house go out and he knew that his father had left the living room to go into the kitchen. There he would make himself a pot of coffee and then sit down and wait for Bruce.

He knew his mother was now upstairs in her bedroom lying in bed and trying to read a novel, the night light a dim glow above her pale face. But she, too, would not go to sleep until he was back home again.

I'm their only son, he thought. And they almost lost me for good. And then he said, maybe they have. Maybe I am lost for good.

"It wasn't a good winter," Dan Warner said.

Now you are left with an only son, Bruce thought. Now Oliver is alone. He has no longer a brother to lend a car to . . . to drive along a dark road on a snowy night.

Oliver is alone, too.

"It wasn't," Bruce said.

The two sat there in silence, two separate figures, and then Bruce opened the door and got out of the car.

"Thanks for the lift, Mr. Warner," he said.

"Glad to do it."

"I'll remember what you said."

"Fine."

"Good night, Mr. Warner."

"Good night, Bruce."

And Bruce started to walk to the house when he heard Dan Warner's voice call to him again.

"Bruce."

He came back to the car.

"I forgot I have something for you."

The man's face hovered between the lamplight and the gloom. A bleak mask.

"For me?"

"Uh-huh."

Dan Warner reached over to the back of the car and then straightened up again. He held out something in his hand.

50

"This is for you."

It was Raymond's floppy hat. Bruce stared at it and a shiver went through him.

"I know Raymond would've liked you to have it. He always said you wanted a hat like this one. That you almost had a . . . a mania for it."

Bruce took the hat.

"It's yours now," Dan Warner said.

He drove off and the last thing Bruce saw was the gleam of the red dome light and then that was gone.

He went into the house holding the hat.

7

He was in the house alone and then he heard the phone ring. His father had gone to his law office in the city and his mother to the little dress shop that she owned in Cordell. The morning was gray and warm, ready for a fierce summer storm. A few raindrops were already falling. He heard the phone ring again, a low, insistent sound.

He was sitting in the kitchen, drinking coffee and casually reading the morning newspaper. He slowly put the paper down and sat there listening to the phone.

It stopped and there was a pause and he heard the clatter of large raindrops against the windows. The phone started ringing again.

This time he got up and went out of the kitchen along the carpeted hallway, footsteps muffled, and into the living room, his eyes fixed upon the gray, lowering sky outside.

He picked up the receiver.

"Hello?"

There was no answer.

"Hello?" he said again.

The summer curtains swayed and circled silently and then he heard the low, mad, mocking laughter.

A feeling of cold despair swept over him.

"Who is it?"

Still the laughter. The wind gusted through the open windows and the curtains shivered and swung and became slack again.

And now fear was threading the despair.

"What do you want of me?"

His voice rose against the clatter of the rain onto glass and the laughter stopped, silence, and then there was a click.

"What?" he whispered.

He stood there holding the receiver in his right hand, his gaze fixed on the gray sky.

His cane lay on the floor.

He slowly began putting the receiver back upon its rest. But his hand was wet and chilled and the black receiver almost slipped from his grasp.

He finally set it down.

He stood there a long time, not closing the windows against the rain, just stood there, and then he stirred himself and turned and went to the stairs. He mounted them, step by step, and then he came to his room. He went inside and shut the door.

Shut it tight so that he would not hear the telephone if it rang again.

But this did not help him.

Not at all.

For in his fevered mind he heard the laughter again. Low, mad, and mocking.

8

The vault box was open. A hand descended slowly and picked up the white sheet of paper that was in the box. Picked it up, held it in the shadowed light, and slowly two words were read aloud in the privacy of the vault booth.

"By fire."

The executioner smiled.

"The first shall die by fire."

The words drifted downward into a well of silence. The smile vanished from the face. Only a mask of cold hatred remained.

The paper was put back into the metal box and the box returned to the shelf of the vault.

"Have a good day," the guard said.

"I will."

When the executioner got outside the bank the sun was still shining brilliantly.

Soon it would be evening.

9

They were sitting in the empty stands. Just the two of them. Bruce Kendall and Ed Millman. The summer evening was coming on, soft and cooling, and Ed had just finished a mile run around the cinder track. Now they sat there, on the lowest level of the stands, Ed in his track suit, mouth open, still trying to get his breath back from his hard run. Bruce leaned forward, hands on knees, a distant, haunted look in his eyes. He wore a T-shirt and an old pair of jeans.

From where they sat they could see the square low form of the locker building. It was a windowless structure of gray bricks. The door had been left open and the fading sunlight gleamed upon the large brass knob.

Ed had hung his clothes on one of the hooks in the empty locker room. He would soon go back there and shower and dress. Bruce gazed sadly at the low building and remembered the times he had spent in the locker room with the rest of the team just before and after a track meet.

He was captain of the team then.

They were the good days, he thought. And now they were over. Smashed to pieces against an old oak tree.

Old and bare of leaves. I never saw it with leaves. I was the best runner of them all. A record holder. The record still stands and they say it will stand for a long time. But I'll never run again. I know that now. The same as that tree will never have leaves again. The leg will never come back into shape. I know that now. They lied to me. The same way they lied to me about my new face. There is no new face. The same as there will never be new leaves on that snowy tree. This morning I looked into the mirror and I saw the outlines of a scar just under my right eye. A tiny scar. But it will come out strong. A ragged, ugly scar. And then there'll be others.

They lied to me. Just to make me feel good.

To give me hope.

And then Ed's voice broke into his thoughts.

"Well, Bruce?"

He had asked Bruce to come out and watch him run. Had stopped by the house and finally persuaded Bruce to come down to the athletic field with him.

You keep to yourself too much. It's not good for you.

I just feel like it these days, Ed.

Well, you shouldn't let it get to you.

Bruce shrugged and was silent.

I saw Marian and she says you don't want to go out with her anymore.

Marian?

And he felt a quiver in his heart.

She says you're angry at her for something.

I'm not.

Then what is it?

It's got nothing to do with her.

Well, what is it?

And he was on point of telling Ed of his fears that bordered on terror, of his despair, but then he closed it down as he did with everyone else.

He said nothing.

Why don't you call her up? We'll go out on a date together. Elaine and me and you and Marian.

Let's leave it alone, he said.

But Bruce, you're too . . .

Will you drop it?

And Ed looked at him and slowly nodded.

Okay. It's dropped. But come on down to the field with me.

I'm not in the mood.

I need help. Need it bad, Bruce.

You don't need me.

Will you do me the favor and come on?

Okay, Bruce finally said, I'll go with you.

"Well?" Ed asked again, leaning over and loosening the laces of his spiked shoes.

Bruce slowly turned to him.

"You're still way out of condition, Ed."

Ed nodded.

"I can feel that. And?"

"Your form was getting pretty lousy the last three hundred yards or so."

"Lousy? As bad as that?"

"Yes. Especially when you came off the last turn."

Ed wiped his glistening forehead with his handkerchief, the rest of his face, and slowly, thoughtfully tucked the handkerchief away.

"What else?"

"Your arms were all wrong. Especially coming down the stretch."

"Too jerky?"

"That's right. You were struggling too much."

"I was."

"You lost all your fluency."

"Fluency?" Ed echoed.

He suddenly leaned back and laughed. Bruce sat

59

there listening to the low, bubbling sound. It warmed him for the moment. Ed's laughter was always pleasant to hear. He always smiled and laughed easily and generously. There was never any malice in his laughter. And Bruce thought, maybe that's why I like him so much.

He listened and later on he was to remember that this was to be the last time. The last time he was ever to hear Ed Millman's laughter.

Edward Joseph Millman.

Son of Harold and Dorothy Millman.

Born January 6, 1962.

"Fluency," Ed said, his laughter softly dying away. "That's the word the coach always likes to use. He's a one-word coach."

"Maybe. But it's the right word this time, Ed."

"And I lost it in the stretch?"

"Yes."

"That's interesting. Real interesting. I'll have to work on it."

"You will. Needs a lot of work. Without fluency you're just another runner."

"I'll buy that."

He pushed back his long black hair and smiled at Bruce. He had the tall, slim build of the distance runner. Clean lines to his body and face. There had always been an easy grace to him. Easy and natural. In the way he moved about and in the way he acted with people. But since the accident it seemed to Bruce that some of the grace had slipped away from him. That underneath it all Ed had become a troubled person.

An anxious one.

It even shows up in his running, Bruce thought. And he used to run so effortlessly.

"Think I'll get my form back, Bruce?"

Bruce smiled at him gently.

60

"I'm sure you will, Ed."

"No doubts?"

"None."

"You're leveling?"

"Yes."

And he said to himself, am I lying to him? And why is he so anxious about his running? He never was that way before. Everything went so easy with him.

"Okay," Ed murmured.

They were silent a while. The day was slowly fading. Bruce spoke.

"But the first thing I'd do is throw away some of those butts you smoke. No good for the wind. No good at all. Especially when you're coming down the home stretch and you've got to give it everything you have."

Ed's face became somber.

"I know, Bruce. I'll have to knock it off. Cold turkey."

"That's the best way. That's how I did it."

"Been smoking too much lately. I used to control it."

"Especially in the track season."

"It . . . it's just that I've been a little nervous and jumpy lately. Kind of uptight. You know what I mean?"

"Yes," Bruce said softly.

"Kind of uptight," Ed said again.

And Bruce looking at him thought, we never talk of that night. Never. Not a single word. Just steer clear of it. Like a ship veering away from a reef which would tear a hole in its keel and wreck it.

"I'm worried, Bruce. A lot of things. You know what I mean?"

Yes, Ed. I know. That night will never leave any of us alone. Never.

"A lot of things. But one of them is that I need a scholarship. Need it badly to get into college and then go on to law school. An athletic scholarship. My old man is not doing too well these days. Money is running short. And there are no summer jobs around anymore."

"You'll get that scholarship, Ed. Just work on your form. You'll get it back again."

"You really think so, Bruce?"

"Yes."

"And you'll come out and help me?"

And he said to himself fiercely, I will, Ed. Damnit, I will help you.

"Sure. You'll get it all back, Ed. And then you'll see how many of the big universities will go after you."

Ed's eyes lit up. He patted Bruce's shoulder affectionately.

"Thanks, Bruce. You make me feel good."

"Then I'm glad I came along with you."

There was a pause and Ed asked gently, "And when are you going to work out again, Bruce?"

Bruce gazed at the clear, concerned eyes and then looked away.

"Soon, Ed," he murmured. "Soon."

Ed saw the fingers tighten over the handle of the cane and he didn't say anything more. The two sat there a long time, each with his own thoughts. A silver plane passed high overhead, flashed against a swathe of murky sky, sped onward till it was gone out of their lives forever, and then all was still and empty again.

The green grass of the infield was slowly darkening.

"I had a strange call last night," Ed said.

"What do you mean?"

"Sort of a weirdo call."

Over at the locker room a shadow angled from the roof to the grass below.

"I was alone," Ed said in a low and absorbed voice.

"And the phone started to ring. I went over to it and picked it up and I said hello but there was no answer. I said it again and I could hear a soft breathing on the other end. Somebody was there."

Bruce felt a chill gradually creep over him.

"I was about to slam down the phone when the voice began to speak. A strange voice. A man's voice."

"Man's?"

"Yes."

"And?"

"It said, Is this Edward Joseph Millman?"

"Your full name?"

"Yes."

Ed's face had become pale and drawn. He tried to laugh but couldn't. He began to speak again.

Bruce listened intently.

"Kind of like an undertaker. Or a preacher. You know what I mean, Bruce? A strange, echoing voice Low and resonant. And every word in place."

"And then?"

"He said, I wish to speak to you, Edward. I have a . . ."

"Go on."

But Ed had stopped talking. He was looking with a fixed gaze at the locker room.

"What is it, Ed?"

Ed gazed and slowly shook his head and smiled weakly.

"Nothing."

"What, Ed?"

"Nothing. Just thought I saw someone go into the locker room. It happened so fast. Almost like a shadow gliding in there."

Bruce had risen and was looking almost fearfully at the building.

63

"It's nothing, Bruce. My nerves are shot."

The door was still open and the brass knob gleamed faintly.

"Maybe there was someone," Bruce said.

Ed shook his head determinedly.

"No. I'm sure of that now."

"Let's go over and check it out."

"Bruce, don't make me feel like a damn fool. I feel lousy enough. Sit down, will you?"

"Are you sure?"

"Damnit, I'm sure."

Bruce slowly sat down again.

"Go on," he finally said.

Ed breathed in and then sighed out low.

"It's got me seeing things."

"Go on, Ed," Bruce said and now his voice was tense and harsh.

Ed stared at him silently and then began to speak again.

"A weirdo call. And it shook me up. You can see what it's done to me." He paused and touched Bruce gently. "Maybe I'd better knock it off."

"What did he say?" Bruce insisted.

Ed shook his head.

"I shouldn't have opened it up at all, Bruce. It was dumb of me."

"Ed, I have to know."

"You look kind of shaky, Bruce. It . . . it goes into that night. I'm dropping it."

"I want to know."

Their eyes met and then Ed looked away from him.

"He said, I have to talk to you about the crime that was committed on that sinful winter night."

"Crime?"

Bruce's hands trembled.

"That's what I said to him. What crime? And he laughed."

"Laughed?"

Bruce's right hand clenched and the nails bit into the flesh.

"A low, weirdo laugh. You know full well what I'm talking about, Edward. It was reported in many newspapers, Edward, and I have read them all. Every detail of the crime. Edward, the wages of sin are death."

"Death?"

Ed didn't seem to hear Bruce's whisper. He went on talking, in a gray monotone, his eyes focused on the evening's lengthening shadows.

He was reliving the experience. Hearing the words still another time.

"The young must give up their sinful drinking, Edward. Or they shall all pay the supreme penalty. Isn't that crystal clear to you Edward? You must repent. And I shall save you. For my lifework is the saving of the young from their sins. I have just come from another part of the country. My task is done there. I have saved and I have punished, as the Lord so decrees. And now I am here. Long delayed but I am here. Repent or die, Edward. Those are my words to you. The words of Reverend William Dunn."

Ed's voice trailed off into the silence.

"William Dunn?"

"Yes."

"Don't you remember him? He was here when we were kids. Don't you, Ed? Reverend Dunn?"

Ed shook his head.

"He was a weirdo. And finally he had to leave the community. Was forced to leave. He got hold of me one day and lashed me for dropping my schoolbooks on the pavement. Said I desecrated them. Made me turn

65

and then lashed me four times. And then my father and your father and . . ."

"I remember," Ed cut in. "It was so long ago I had forgotten."

"I never did," Bruce murmured.

They were silent.

"So now he's back," Ed said.

Bruce turned to him.

"Maybe it's not him at all. Maybe it's somebody with a crazy sense of humor. Kind of sick. One of our nutty friends. We have some, you know."

"We have," Ed said quietly.

"Well?"

"You know that's not the answer, Bruce."

"I know," Bruce said hopelessly.

"This man is for real. I can feel it in my bones. And something is bugging him bad."

"Did he say he'd call again?"

"No."

"Just hung up?"

"Just that. And then silence."

Bruce sat there rigid, the sweat cold and damp on his body. Then he heard Ed's voice as if coming from a great distance.

"For real," Ed said. "And it shook me up. I was alone in the house and there was no one to talk to."

He calls when we're alone, Bruce thought. How does he know that? Does he watch our houses? Does he follow us? Is he the one who's been . . . ?

And then Ed was speaking again.

"I took out one of my father's bottles of Scotch and had a stiff drink. But that didn't settle me down. I was thinking of going off to Carlson's just to be with somebody. And then I remembered that he's been closed up. Out of business. Strange, the things you forget when you're knocked off balance. Your mind plays so many tricks on you. You feel so lost."

I know the feeling well, Bruce thought bitterly.

"I was alone. I thought of going over to see Dan Warner."

"The police?"

"I figured I ought to tell him. I guess I was scared, Bruce."

"And did you?"

Ed shook his head.

"No. Why bring back memories? He has so much to forget. So damned much."

"He has," Bruce whispered. "We all have."

Ed turned and looked at Bruce's pale and agonized face.

"Christ, I don't know why I told you this," he said. "You've got to forgive me, Bruce. Please."

"Nothing to forgive."

"It was wrong."

"No."

"I . . . I just had to tell someone. It shook me up. And we're so close, Bruce."

"You told me. And you should have. I made you tell me."

"But now I've opened up that night for you. I've put you back into it. It's the last thing I ever wanted to do, Bruce."

"I never left that night," Bruce said.

They sat in silence, motionless and alone, until Ed slowly rose.

"I'd better take my shower before I start tightening up. I'll be out in no time. And then I'll drive you home."

"Okay, Ed," Bruce murmured.

"Be out in no time."

But Ed stood there, not going on to the shadowed building. Just stood there looking down at his friend, a gentle, sad light in his eyes.

We have known each other since childhood, Bruce thought. As long as I knew Raymond. And Raymond is gone forever.

Ray will never come back and wear his floppy hat again.

"I'm absent-minded as hell lately," Ed said.

"We all get that way sometimes," Bruce said.

"I forget things all over the place. It's not like me."

"It will pass."

Ed nodded and still stood there.

"Yes. I guess so."

"Stop worrying about the future. It will take care of itself."

A breeze ruffled Ed's hair and he put his hand up to it and straightened it out, a delicate, graceful gesture and then the hand fell to his side awkwardly.

"I'll stop worrying," he said.

Bruce knew that Ed didn't want to leave him. And he felt the same way. Wanted Ed to stay there and talk more.

Talk about anything. Just so he stayed a little longer in front of him. Tall and clean-featured against the coming night.

It was strange. So very strange. As if both had a premonition . . . a dark premonition . . . dark and shattering.

"Don't forget about the lock, Ed," he heard himself say and he wondered why he was saying it.

"The lock?"

"The one on the locker-room door."

Ed smiled.

"Oh. You're right. I'd better remember to shut the . . ." And then he hesitated and corrected himself.

"I mean *not* to shut the door. Not to shut it from the inside or I'll never get out of that damned room."

"Now you got it," Bruce smiled.

"It's time they fixed that lousy lock. Fixed it for good or got a new one."

"It's going to be a new one. But not until the fall term."

"That's the school system for you."

"Lots of red tape in all bureaucracies. Red tape and forms to fill out."

"And be approved. Even for a lock. Always a hassle."

"I was once stuck in there for an hour," Bruce said. "And then the coach came along and opened it with a key from the outside. It works fine from the outside."

"But it's death from the inside," Ed said.

Bruce never forgot those words.

"We'll make sure the next lock they put on that door isn't a snap lock," he said.

"You can bet your last dollar it will be," Ed said.

He stood there smiling down at Bruce but deep in his eyes there was that haunting, sad look.

"I'm sorry I shook you up, Bruce," he said quietly.

"I told you to forget it."

Ed raised his hand over his head and then turned away.

"I'll see you."

"See you," Bruce said softly.

He watched the tall, slender figure walk across the grass and into the shadow of the locker room and disappear.

The brass knob on the open door gleamed.

10

He had been sitting there, lost in thought and memory, and he never knew and never would know how much time had passed. But he never forgot the instant he looked up and out of his swirling inner world and saw that the door to the locker room was shut.

And this brought him to his feet.

Why had Ed shut the door?

Why?

The only way to open that door now was with a key. And Ed had the key in his clothes. So why did he shut the door?

Now it could only be opened from the outside.

And the key was in his clothes.

In his clothes.

Bruce began walking across the grass, the thoughts whirling in his mind, whirling and repeating themselves when he heard a distant, muffled cry.

His name was in the core of that cry.

Bruce shivered and dropped his cane and began to run desperately across the grass. Each time he came down on his bad leg a pain seared through him and brought hot tears of agony to his eyes. But he grimly ran on and as he neared the building he heard Ed's muffled voice more distinctly.

"Bruce . . . Bruce . . ."

It was a gasping, pleading call for help.

"Ed."

The acrid smell of smoke came to him and he could see gray wisps curling out and through the crevices of the locked door.

"Ed!"

The cry now came from the depths of his being.

"Ed!" he shouted again.

The brass knob turned and rattled as if in frantic answer. Bruce smashed against the door with all his strength. The door shuddered but would not give. The knob rattled again but this time weakly and then it suddenly stopped and was at rest. Bruce could almost feel Ed's hand falling away from the knob.

"Ed!"

He flung his body against the door again and again. A panic set in over him and he was about to weep when he remembered the fire ax that hung in a narrow glass case a few yards to the right of the doorway. He rushed over to it and searched wildly about for the small metal hammer used to break the glass. But it was not hanging in its accustomed place. Somebody had taken it away.

Bruce clenched his fist and smashed it through the glass, shattering it into gleaming fragments. He felt the sharp, jagged pain pierce through him and the warm blood streaming over his hand. He grabbed the ax from its rack and ran back to the closed door.

With fierce, savage strokes he finally broke his way into the smoke-filled room.

"Ed!" he cried out and began gasping for air.

He went farther into the room, the smoke enveloping him.

"Ed!"

He felt his lungs bursting and his eyes stinging.

"Edddd!"

His foot touched something soft and yielding. He dropped to his knees and saw the glimmering face and the white body still wet and glistening from the shower.

He's still alive, he said to himself.

"Ed."

Alive. Alive.

Bruce put his arms under the silent body and then lifted up with all his remaining strength, the blood still streaming from his hand.

"You'll . . . be . . . all . . . right," he gasped soothingly.

He said it over and over again, like a mad litany.

"All . . . right . . . all . . . right . . . all . . . right . . ."

He staggered his way through the smoke, gasping and coughing, and then out into the life-giving air.

He walked onto the grass still carrying Ed. He stopped and stood stock-still.

"The key, Ed?"

He said it again, in a plaintive voice.

"Where's the key?"

His knees buckled under him but still he held tightly in his arms the glimmering white body of his friend.

Held it tightly. Fiercely protecting it from death.

And then a blackness overwhelmed him.

11

He dreamed and in his dream he was running on the track with Ed at his side and suddenly Ed said to him, There's Raymond, and sure enough just ahead of them at the first big turn was Raymond wearing his floppy hat and running with an easy lope.

I thought he was dead, Ed said.

I thought so, too, Bruce said.

Let's go after him and find out.

We'll catch up to him and ask him.

They both began to run as fast as they could after Raymond. But no matter how fast they ran, Raymond seemed to go faster, the floppy hat bobbing up and down, up and down on his head.

Raymond, stop, will you, Bruce called out.

He doesn't want us to catch up to him, Ed said.

Let's go faster.

I'm going as fast as I can.

Faster.

Okay.

Bring your arms up more, Ed. Your form's terrible.

How's it now?

Fine.

We don't seem to be gaining on him.

Faster. Faster.

Faster.

They went around the track again and again, never tiring and never seeming to catch up to Raymond. Without a word of warning Ed put on a tremendous burst of speed and left Bruce behind. He caught up to Raymond and Raymond turned and grinned at him without breaking stride and the two of them ran together, side by side.

Wait for me, Bruce called out.

But they ran on.

Please. Please wait.

They ran on.

Please don't leave me alone. It's getting so dark. So dark and cold.

They ran on.

Wait for me. Please. I'm afraid to be alone. I'm afraid of being alone in the dark. Alone in the dark.

They stopped and turned to him. They motioned him to come up to them. A bright, welcoming smile on their faces.

He laughed out in joy and ran like a soft wind, graceful, floating strides and just as he was about to reach them . . .

He awoke.

12

He awoke and he saw his mother sitting in a chair beside the bed. She got up and came over to him.

"How do you feel, Bruce?"

He didn't answer. He saw his father standing by one of the open windows. The sun was just coming up and he knew that he had been in the hospital all night.

"They say you'll be able to go home now."

"That's right, Bruce," his father said.

Bruce looked at his bandaged hand and didn't speak.

"They had to put some stitches in your hand, Bruce," his father said. "But the hand will be fine."

"Yes," his mother nodded.

"How is Ed?" Bruce asked.

His mother looked over to his father.

"How is he?" Bruce asked again.

"He's dead," his father said.

Bruce slowly closed his eyes and tried to dream.

But it was no use.

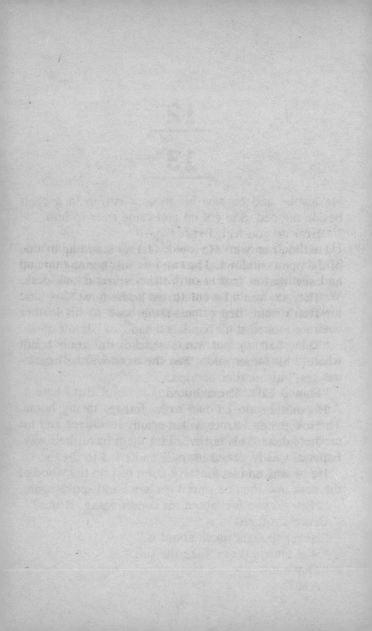

13

He sat in Dan Warner's office at police headquarters. The day was bright and hot and now a breeze came up and rustled the papers on Warner's broad oak desk. Warner got up and went to the nearest window and lowered it and then came slowly back to his leather chair.

His lean, strong face was thoughtful and somber. But when he spoke his voice was casual and almost pleasant.

"Should have air conditioning in here. But I hate it. And what I hate I don't have. Except in my home. There I give in to things. Especially to Oliver and his mother when she was alive. I let them have their way. Especially Oliver these days."

He paused and let his large palm rest on the wood of the desk and then he raised his hand and spoke again.

"How do you feel about air conditioning, Bruce?"

Bruce shrugged.

"Never thought much about it."

"Was always there. Like the sun."

"That's it."

"And?"

The police eyes scanned Bruce. Seemed ever to be studying him.

"I suppose I like it."

Warner smiled.

"So does Oliver. That's why we have it in the house. All you young fellows were brought up on air conditioning."

And Bruce wanted to say, Raymond liked it, too. You considered him, too, didn't you when you went out and air-conditioned your house? Didn't you, Mr. Warner? But Bruce noted that he never mentioned Raymond anymore. There was a picture of Mrs. Warner, who was now dead six years, and of Oliver, who was still alive, on Warner's desk. Both in gilt frames. Both placed at angles to the leather chair, so that he could always see them.

But no picture of Raymond anywhere in the office. Bruce was sure that there was no longer any trace of Raymond in the house. Warner had even gotten rid of the floppy hat.

He has so damned much to forget, Ed had once said.

"Oliver is spoiled. All you young ones are spoiled," Warner said gently. "But I guess you're all right."

He smiled at Bruce and yet in the back of the steady gray eyes there was no warmth. Bruce had been more than an hour with the man and all the time, underneath Warner's formal concern and outward pleasantness . . . underneath it all, Bruce felt there was an icy hostility toward him.

A hatred that the man kept leashed within.

"Maybe we are spoiled," Bruce said. "But we try to be decent. I find that most of us do try."

"Decent in an indecent world. Is that it?"

"You could call it that."

"So my generation kind of loused things up for you."

"If you want to put it that way."

80

Warner grunted, then leaned forward and selected an old pipe from a rack of pipes on his desk. Bruce remembered Oliver buying the rack for his father as a birthday present. And Oliver's odd remark, "Don't know what to get the old failure for his birthday." And Bruce's look of astonishment and Oliver's loud and almost harsh laughter. An amused, wild gleam in the often placid blue eyes.

Warner filled the pipe, tamped the tobacco down with a big thumb, and then lit the pipe and puffed. The first tiny cloud of smoke sent a cold tremor through Bruce. He turned his eyes away from the smoke, which made him think of Ed's glimmering face. He was certain that Warner was aware of his reaction. And knew full well the reason for it.

Warner puffed and leaned back in his chair. A solid block of a man.

The door of the room was closed but Bruce could still hear the muffled sound of a typewriter and the murmur of voices. Through the windows he could see the green of the lawn and the leafy tree standing motionless in the center and the car traffic on the main street of Cordell.

He heard Warner speak again, in a low, clear voice.

"When I was young I did a few years of professional boxing. Light heavyweight. And when you come upon a fighter whose style puzzled you, a southpaw especially, you would say, I find it hard to read him. Ever hear that expression, Bruce?"

Bruce shook his head.

"I don't think so."

And then he remembered vaguely that someone sometime back had used that expression with him.

Someone close to him.

Raymond.

But he couldn't remember when or why.

"Can't read him. That's what we used to say. Comes

from the fight game. I wasn't a bad light heavyweight. Considering the talent around then I could've gone very far. Maybe even to a title bout. But then I gave it up and settled down."

He paused and a soft, reflective look came over the rugged face.

"I met the girl who was to become my wife and Oliver's mother and I settled down. Got into police work."

Bruce waited, for he knew that the man had not come to his point.

"Can't read him. That's what we used to say. Or he's hard to read." The reflective look faded out. The face became impassive. "Well, Bruce, I find all you young ones, fellows and girls together, find you very hard to read."

He leaned forward.

"I don't know what in the hell you want or are trying to get from life."

There was a soft, tentative knock on the door and Warner called out in curt answer. The door opened and a policeman came in with a paper in his hand. He went over to Warner without glancing at Bruce and stood there while his chief read the document and abruptly signed it.

"Keep him there. No matter how hard his parents holler."

"Yes, Dan."

The policeman left the room, closing the door behind him.

"That was one of your schoolmates," Warner said. "Drunk and disorderly. Broke a store window on Chester Street. I'm putting him in a cell this time. How does that sit with you, Bruce?"

Bruce didn't answer.

"Well?"

He knew the man was challenging him.

"Okay with me, Mr. Warner. But don't you think it's better to try to find out why we're doing so much drinking? It's not just here in Cordell. It's all over the country."

"I'm a policeman."

But you're also a father, Bruce thought.

"Can't read any of you anymore," Warner said gruffly.

He took the pipe out of his mouth and set it down on an ashtray with a cold and deliberate motion.

When he spoke his voice was hard and final.

"No, Bruce. While we've been talking of other things I've been thinking of Ed Millman and his death. Going over in my mind everything you said to me. I've been digesting it."

"It's not what you think, Mr. Warner. I keep telling you that."

Warner shook his head.

"Ed Millman's death was caused by negligence. His and the school's. I'd say criminal negligence on the school's part."

Bruce was about to speak but Warner motioned him to be silent.

"That lock should've been replaced long ago. But that's one aspect of the case. The other and most damning of all is that Ed smoked. You know that he did. And you said to me that he did. Couldn't control it, you said that, Bruce."

"Yes, but . . ."

Warner rode quietly over him.

"He smoked. The fire was caused by a cigarette dropped into a wastebasket. Ed thought he had put it out but the cigarette was still burning."

"I told you I know that Ed did not smoke in there."

"How do you know?"

Bruce hesitated before speaking.

"I . . . I just know."

Warner shook his head grimly.

"You don't."

"Well, I feel . . ."

"Feelings never count for much in police work. Facts do. Let me give you the facts again. He had a cigarette before he took off his track suit. He went in to take a shower and then the fire started and the smoke filled the room. He tried to get out but the door was shut. Shut because he absent-mindedly shut it."

"He didn't shut the door."

"You told me that Ed was anxious and distraught. Didn't you?"

"Yes, but . . ."

"He was worried about the scholarship. The phone call. So it's logical, isn't it, that he would forget about the lock on the door? Isn't it?"

"But I tell you that's not how it all happened."

"Bruce, that's how the fire department says it happened. And that's how my department sees it. A cigarette tossed into a wastebasket. Hundreds of fires have been caused that way."

"You're wrong. All of you," Bruce cried out.

"Bruce, I listened to you. I took time to think about what you said. And that's my decision."

"But what about the phone call?"

"We can't seem to find Reverend Dunn. Or anybody who has seen or heard of him. Not a trace of the man."

"Ed wasn't lying to me. He got the call."

"I'll keep looking. And even if I do find him, what does it prove?"

"That someone got into the room."

"Now, Bruce . . ."

"Started the fire and went out, closing the door behind him."

"Why a him? Why not a her?"

Bruce felt the man was beginning to mock him.

"Someone did it," he said.

Warner looked wearily over to him.

"You still believe that?"

"Yes. Yes."

"That Reverend Dunn set out to deliberately murder Ed Millman. Set out and was able to do it."

"That's the only way it could have happened. The only way," Bruce said fiercely.

"And just what is the reverend's motive?"

"Motive?"

"People have motives before they murder, Bruce. Reasons for killing other human beings. And whenever you examine them they turn out to be very good reasons—that is, from the point of view of the murderer."

Bruce hesitated and then spoke in a low, tortured voice.

"He wanted us to pay for the crime we committed that night. He called the accident a crime."

Warner's face had turned gray. His big hand clenched and then unclenched.

"Bruce, listen to me," he said. "I'll never say this to you again. I don't want ever to hear of that night. I opened it up to you that time because of Carlson. To warn you to stay away from him. Now I don't want you ever to go into it again with me. Is that clear to you?"

"But . . ."

"Is it?"

His voice rang out like a rifle shot.

"Yes," Bruce said.

They sat there in a well of silence. A gentle breeze shook the leaves of the tree outside on the lawn and then the leaves were still again.

There was a knock on the door and Warner called

out angrily, "Don't disturb me," and then he sat back in his chair and closed his eyes as if in pain.

When he opened them again, he looked over to Bruce and his own face was softer.

"I know how you feel, Bruce," he said. "Everybody appreciates what you did. How you risked your own life trying to save Ed. We all know that." He paused and went on, "But let the police department take care of what it has to take care of. And respect the fire department's findings. It's a good fire department and it has a fine record."

"But I tell you Ed Millman was murdered."

Warner waved his hand at Bruce almost in despair.

"It's a theory and I've looked into it."

"Have you?"

The words were torn out of Bruce's being. He didn't know why he said them. As he saw the face before him become tight and grim, the eyes savagely cold, the lips thin into a sharp line, he knew he shouldn't have said them.

"Just what do you mean by that?"

Bruce didn't answer.

"I'm asking you again."

Warner had risen from his chair.

"I don't know why I said it, Mr. Warner."

"But you did."

"I don't know why," Bruce mumbled.

Warner still stood there, a dark figure blocking out the sight of the green tree and the bright sunlight. Even the sound of the traffic was now dim and lost to Bruce.

Warner began to speak in a steady, harsh voice.

"I know how much you've been through," he said. "But I'll be damned if I let anybody talk to me that way. I never have and never will. Are you questioning my integrity as a police officer?"

"No," Bruce said.

"Good. There's the door. Use it. And don't ever come to me again."

Bruce got up and stared at the stony figure facing him and then he turned and went out of the office, closing the door behind him.

Warner slowly sat down, his face tight and impassive. He sat there motionless. Finally, he pressed the button of his office intercom.

"Edith?"

"Yes, Mr. Warner?"

"I don't want any more visitors."

"But you have an appointment with the . . ."

"Cancel it," he said curtly. "I don't want to see anyone for a while."

"Yes, Mr. Warner."

He sat there a long time in a ringing silence, a lone man in an empty room. He bent over and opened a lower drawer of his desk and took out a gilt-framed picture. He set it on his desk directly in front of him.

He looked at it steadily. Then his lips opened in pain.

"Raymond," he whispered. "They killed you, my son. They killed you."

Two tears trickled down his seamed face. He buried his head in his arms.

But when he put the picture back into his desk drawer, his face had turned hard as flint and his eyes glinted with a fierce and mad stare.

14

The ceremony was simple and poignant. Toward its end Oliver came over and stood by him. Oliver was grave and mournful and it seemed to Bruce that he had lost some weight since the last time he had seen him.

The ceremony came to its end, the sad words ceased, and the people began to move out of the crowded chapel. Some still lingered behind in murmuring clusters.

"Elaine is taking it hard," Oliver said in a low voice.

Bruce looked to where Elaine Ross was still sitting, her head bowed and her body shaking with sobs. Her mother stood by helplessly.

"They were pretty close to each other," he said. "Ed and . . . she . . ."

Bruce's voice trembled and he stopped speaking. He wondered why Oliver had made it a point to note Elaine's grief and to speak of it to him. Oliver knew how close Elaine and Ed had been.

Bruce thought of Elaine sleeping in Ed's arms in the back of the car, the dark, snowy night all about them.

And ahead of them at the side of the road, the dark oak tree.

Waiting, waiting for all of them.

"Are you going to the cemetery?" Oliver asked.

"Yes," Bruce said.

"I never liked open graves," Oliver said. "I'll pass this one up."

He straightened his narrow black tie and smiled gently with his quiet eyes and went over to Ed Millman's parents. They were of medium size and he stood over them tall and rangy, his handsome face with its straight and small features now pale and drawn. And Bruce watching the little group thought for the first time how full of contradictions Oliver was. Such small features for a tall person. The black hair, the pale white forehead directly underneath, and the placid blue eyes that could be so deceptive at times. The wild, amused gleam that would suddenly set into them. And at that instant Bruce remembered what Raymond had once said bitterly to him, Oliver can be hard to read. That's an expression my father uses. It means he's hard to make out. And there are some lousy times when you just can't make Oliver out, no way. He gets under your skin and his eyes are laughing at you.

Bruce now wondered why Raymond had spoken so bitterly of his brother that evening. They had been sitting in Carlson's, the two of them. What had Oliver done to him? Raymond never told him and never again spoke of his brother in that harsh way.

Raymond loved Oliver.

And Oliver loved him.

Bruce saw Oliver bend over and kiss Ed's mother on the cheek, comfort her with his long, tender arm about her and he saw her burst into tears again.

Bruce put his hand to his eyes and walked out of the shadowy chapel into the bright summer day.

He heard his mother speak gently to him.

"You'll sit with us, Bruce."

"All right," he said.

"We'll be leaving in a few minutes," his father murmured. "That limousine over there. Third one in the cortege, Bruce."

His father's eyes were misty behind the gold-rimmed glasses. He's really a good man, Bruce thought. They both have been pretty good to me all my life. And I've brought them so much heartache and despair.

"Okay, Dad," he said.

He wanted to say more but he didn't. He wondered why it was so hard to tell his father what was in his heart. To open up to his mother.

Who had put the wall between them?

Was there really a wall?

Why didn't he ever try to find out?

"Okay, Dad," he said again.

His father patted him tenderly and moved off with his mother.

Bruce stood there, looking about him and not seeing anybody and then he saw Janet Stoner, who was Raymond's girl friend. Bruce had not seen her since the day she came to visit him in the hospital.

She came slowly and deliberately over to him.

"I've been wanting to talk to you, Bruce."

He nodded and gazed at her. She had dark auburn hair and her features had sharpened since Raymond's death. Her liquid black eyes had become large and fierce. Before the death they had blended into the face but now they had become its outstanding feature.

He thought with a pang how much she had suffered.

"Ed is gone now. Isn't he?" she said in a low, fervid voice.

"Yes," he whispered.

"And I don't feel sorry for him."

He stared at her.

"Janet . . ."

She shook her head bitterly.

"No. Not for him. And not for you or anybody in that damned car."

"Let it alone," he said softly and desperately.

"No. No."

He turned to walk away from her but she grasped his arm tightly.

"You all deserve to die. All of you."

"Janet, for Christ's sake . . ."

"You are all murderers."

He turned his face from her sharply as if she had struck him. Her fingers were tight about his wrist, in a grasp of steel.

"You all will pay. If there is any justice in this world. Each and every one of you. I can see it. Yes, I can."

"Janet," he said, "I've already paid. I'll never stop paying. Let me alone."

Her black eyes blazed with hatred.

"It's not over yet, Bruce. There is a God in this world. A God of justice and of bitter vengeance. It's not over."

She released his hand and turned and walked swiftly away from him.

15

At the cemetery he understood what Oliver meant and he knew that he couldn't face the open grave. Could not stand there and see the fine grains of dark earth come raining down upon Ed till it obliterated him.

He just couldn't stand there and watch it happen.

So he threaded his way silently through the large group of mourners until he found himself at the very edge of the gathering.

He stood there under the branch of a tree, head bowed, off by himself. He could no longer hear the words distinctly. They were like whisperings in the dazzling sunshine.

He was alone with his somber thoughts.

And gradually, subtly, he became aware of a figure standing next to him. He had sensed no motion nor had heard any movement, but the figure was there.

"Hello, Bruce."

He shivered and his hand closed about the grip of his cane and he looked up and into a lean. haggard face with large glowing hazel eyes.

"So Edward Millman is gone."

A long, lean man, well over six feet, dressed in a black suit. He held an old white panama straw hat in one of his large, bony hands. He was about forty years old but his head was bald and it shone in the sun.

"I'm Reverend William Dunn."

"Yes," Bruce sighed out.

Above them the sky was high and vast. And all about them was a wide, pervading silence, save for the whispering words, whispering from the distant open grave.

"I am here, Bruce Kendall."

The eyes were the eyes of a cat. Glowing and impenetrable.

"What do you want of me?"

"Just to stand by you. In your time of need."

"Leave me alone."

"I left you alone once before. Was forced to leave you alone. And now look at what has happened to you."

"Please."

"Let us now be quiet and listen to the closing words of the awesome ceremony," the man said in a low, throbbing voice.

"What do you want of me?" Bruce pleaded.

The man lifted one finger high.

"Do not desecrate the dead, Bruce Kendall. Stand and listen."

But it was impossible from where they stood to hear the words clearly. And yet Reverend Dunn did not move from the spot.

Not one inch closer to the open grave.

"We must not miss a word," he said, his face haggard and austere.

There was the sound of a thin and fading scream and Bruce knew that it came from Ed Millman's mother and he sensed that the coffin was being lowered into the enveloping earth.

Reverend Dunn began to speak.

"Edward Millman did not repent. So he paid the penalty."

"You made him pay the penalty," Bruce said.

"He is dead. May peace come to his soul."

"You killed him," Bruce cried out in a low, agonized voice.

The man looked down silently at Bruce, a glint of amusement in the hazel eyes. The lips were thin and bloodless.

"You did it," Bruce said.

The lips opened, slowly, deliberately.

"I?"

"Yes. Yes."

The man shook his bald head side to side and then spoke in a low, severe voice.

"He didn't repent, Bruce. I saw him walk into a bar in town. I warned him to repent. But he was stiff-necked. As stiff-necked as the tribes of Israel. Do you read your Bible, Bruce?"

"You're mad," Bruce said.

And he turned away from the glowing eyes and wanted to shout to the gathered people that here at his side stood Ed's murderer.

But all heads were averted from him, all concentrated upon Ed's grave.

And then he heard his own words flung back at him.

"You are the mad one, Bruce Kendall. No, my boy. I am not a murderer. I am a savior. A savior of souls."

Bruce stood there, rooted to the ground. Held there by the fervid, hypnotic eyes. The voice began again, striking cold terror within him.

"You are the mad one. The doomed one."

"Go away," Bruce whispered.

The bald head shook side to side.

"I am here."

"Why did you come back? Why?"

"To save you. I have been over the country far and wide. Saving the young from themselves. That is my mission in this life."

"You don't save," Bruce said bitterly. "You destroy."

The man raised his finger high.

"No. I wait patiently. Wait for the return of the sinner. But even the Lord's patience has its limits. Is that not so?"

"You kill," Bruce said.

The man stood there, tall and rigid, gazing down at Bruce as from a great height. And suddenly a soft, gentle look came over the man's haggard face.

"Listen to me, my son."

The hazel eyes were now mellow. He put his hand to Bruce's cheek and touched it and the fingers were like fire. Bruce still stood there, powerless to leave the spot.

"Listen to me. Do you think that with a new face you can put on a new character? Until you repent your ways, you are the same sinner as before."

The long, searing fingers slowly left Bruce's face. There was a vast, hypnotic silence. All was still about Bruce, still and frozen in motion. No sound came from the grave. No sound from the ranks of the mourners.

Then the thin, bloodless lips opened again.

"Repent," Reverend William Dunn intoned in a deep, throbbing voice. "Repent or you shall pay for your crime. Pay most dearly. It is gone out of my hands, Bruce Kendall. It is in the hands of you and of the Lord."

Then the man abruptly swung about and strode away and the last Bruce saw of him was the black of the figure and the flash of the sun on the white panama hat, gripped tightly in his hand.

16

He was sitting in his room looking out the window at the darkening sky when he heard the footsteps of his father come to the threshold.

He turned about questioningly. His father adjusted his glasses.

"Bruce?"

"Yes?"

"Mind if I step in for a few minutes?"

"Sure."

His father came in and sat down on one of the chairs. Bruce leaned forward and turned on a lamp. The glow spread over the two figures and onto the small carpet.

"It was a bad day," Mr. Kendall said.

Bruce nodded silently. On one of the walls he could see the shadow of his father's head. He looked at it and not at his father.

"Ed's folks took it rather hard."

"Yes," Bruce murmured.

Mr. Kendall sighed softly and didn't speak. He was a neat, slender man with straight blond hair that was beginning to thin out. He wore a tan polo shirt and brown slacks. He was always careful about how he dressed, Bruce thought. Always tried to look younger than he was. He had been a good tennis player in college and he still played and carefully watched his diet and figure. But there were the beginnings of a little pot about his waist and he was quite sensitive about it.

Yet Bruce remembered him smiling one day and patting his stomach and saying rather ruefully, I'm really becoming your old man.

Bruce used to enjoy playing tennis with his father. They were hard, silent games. And after the match was over they gave each other a few pleasant words and then each went his separate way. And Bruce thinking of it now and waiting for his father to get to the point of his visit, wondered why it always happened that way. In almost everything they did together.

We got close to each other and yet never did.

Never.

Mr. Kendall broke the silence.

"I was downtown and I ran into Dan Warner," he said.

Bruce waited.

"We stopped and chatted."

"And that's why you're here," Bruce said.

His father flushed and shifted his position in his chair.

"Yes, Bruce. I thought I'd go over with you a few things he said to me."

"About Ed and his death?"

Mr. Kendall hesitated and then nodded.

"Yes. That's what we talked about."

There was again the silence. Bruce could hear the low, even sound of the television set coming from the living room downstairs. His mother was watching one of her favorite television programs.

A game show.

She cried at Ed's funeral and now she's watching a game show, he thought cynically. And then he crushed the thought. Why shouldn't she? Life goes on, doesn't it? What do I want her to do? Sit around in black for a month? What the hell's happening to me?

He suddenly heard himself speak and his voice was low and tense.

"Dan Warner thinks I'm a little out of my skull," Bruce said. "Is that it?"

"No, Bruce. Not at all."

"And he wants me to keep my mouth shut. Not to make waves."

"Bruce."

"He doesn't go along with me. I know he doesn't."

Mr. Kendall leaned forward and put his hand on his son's knee.

"Bruce," he said gently, "the police department and the fire department have looked into the matter very thoroughly. Why don't you accept their findings?"

"Because they're wrong," Bruce said.

He saw a look of despair come over his father's mild face. He saw him straighten the glasses on his nose and Bruce felt sorry for him.

Sorry and bitterly angry. Angry at the weakness of the man. Always with the establishment. Always and always.

Like a programmed sheep.

"They're wrong, that's all," he said harshly. "So damned wrong that it's not even funny. They're a bunch of damned fools."

"But the evidence shows that . . ."

"The hell with the evidence," Bruce cut in. "I know what happened and I told Warner what happened and he . . . Oh, what the hell's the use of going into it?"

"Because it's not helping you any."

"What do you mean by that?"

His father hesitated and then spoke.

"Mom and I are very concerned about your

99

. . . your mental and emotional . . ." He looked at Bruce and didn't go on.

"You think I'm cracking up?"

"I . . . I didn't say that."

"But you practically did."

"No, Bruce."

"You did," Bruce said fiercely.

Mr. Kendall rose from his chair.

"Bruce, please listen to me. I . . ."

"No. You listen to me. Warner laughs at Reverend Dunn. Laughs him away. For what reasons I don't know yet. But I have an idea. A damned good one."

"What idea? What are you talking about?"

"Dan Warner doesn't want to get to the bottom of this murder. Nor does he want anybody else to. I know that."

His father moved back just a bit, an anxious, fearful look on his face.

"What?"

"That's right."

"Bruce, how can you say a thing like that?"

"He can't find Reverend Dunn. Nobody can. So he says."

Mr. Kendall nodded slowly, his eyes still fearful.

"That's right. He told me that."

"Well, I've got news for you," Bruce cried out. "Reverend William Dunn found me."

Mr. Kendall's mouth dropped open. He stared at Bruce. The outlines of his shadow were sharp and still on the wall. Then they wavered.

He finally was able to speak.

"Found you?"

Bruce's eyes gleamed triumphantly.

"At the cemetery today. He came and talked to me."

"Talked . . . to you?"

"Yes. Yes. I was standing in the back of the crowd,

away from everybody, under a tree. And he came and stood by me."

Mr. Kendall's face had turned pale. He trembled.

"Bruce."

"What's wrong?"

"You say he talked to you? Stood there and talked to you?"

"Yes."

"But I . . . I turned and looked for you and saw you standing under the tree."

"Well?"

There were tiny beads of perspiration glistening on his father's white forehead.

"You were standing alone, Bruce. Alone."

"He was there, I tell you."

"But . . ."

Bruce's voice rose to a shout.

"Are you trying to tell me that I didn't see him and talk to him?"

"I'm just trying to. . . "

"Are you?" Bruce cut in

"Bruce, will you let me speak?"

His father put his hand out pleadingly and Bruce slapped it away from him.

"To hell with you."

"Bruce!"

They both turned. Mrs. Kendall was standing in the doorway, pale and shaken. She stared from one to the other silently.

"Arthur," she said.

He came to her quickly.

"It's nothing, Nancy. Nothing. Please . . ."

But she looked away from him to Bruce.

"What's wrong here?" she asked and her voice broke. "What?"

"It's nothing, Mom," Bruce said.

"But it is, Bruce. It is."

He gazed at her agonized face and suddenly he swung back upon his father. When he spoke his voice was full of fury and heartbreak.

"You turned once. When he wasn't there. And on that you accuse me of being crazy? Of seeing things that weren't there? Of talking to hallucinations?"

"I didn't say you were crazy, Bruce."

"Goddamnit, you did."

"I didn't say that," his father shouted.

"You did."

"Bruce, goddamnit, Reverend Dunn's dead. Dead."

"What?" Bruce whispered.

"Dan Warner told me that. Dead. Killed in an airplane crash. Two years ago."

"Dan Warner is a liar. I saw the Reverend Dunn. I spoke to him. He's a liar."

"Bruce."

"Arthur, please."

Mr. Kendall turned to her.

"All right, Nancy," he breathed out.

Then Bruce saw them leave the room and go down stairs. When he turned back to the wall, the shadow of his father was gone from it

And he felt alone, so terribly alone and lost

17

The vault box was open. A hand descended slowly and picked up the white sheet of paper that was in the box. Picked it up, held it in the dim light, and slowly two words were read aloud in the privacy of the vault booth.

"By water."

The executioner smiled.

"The second shall die by water."

The words drifted downward into a well of silence. The smile vanished from the face. Now only a mask of cold hatred remained.

The paper was put back into the metal box and the box returned to the shelf of the vault.

"Have a good day," the guard said.

"I will."

When the executioner got outside the bank it had begun to rain.

A cold, drizzling rain.

18

He wanted to talk to Elaine Ross but she wasn't in when he phoned.

"This Bruce Kendall?" her father asked.

"Yes. Mr. Ross."

"How do you feel?"

"Okay, I guess."

"That's good. She's down at the dock fiddling around with her boat, Bruce."

"Oh."

"Think you might drop down there to see her?"

"Yes, Mr. Ross."

"Good. I know this is a kind of hard thing to say to you. But could you try to cheer her up a bit? You know what I mean, Bruce."

"Yes, Mr. Ross. I know."

"Do your best. I'd appreciate it."

"Sure."

"Well, good talking to you. Give my regards to your folks."

"I will."

And he was about to hang up when he heard Mr. Ross's voice again.

"Bruce?"

"Yes?"

"Do me a favor and remind her that we're going over to her aunt's at six tonight."

"Six."

"That's it. Tell her to try to be home an hour before that."

"Okay, Mr. Ross."

"Thanks again, Bruce. Good-bye."

"Good-bye, Mr. Ross."

He put the phone down and gazed through the window. The rain had stopped and the sunlight was just coming through. He got up, took his cane, and went out of the house. The leaves of the trees were wet and the trunks black and glistening.

When he got to the dock, the day had become hot and brilliant. He walked along the gray planking, his footsteps hollow and resonant against the stillness, and then he saw her sitting on a piling, gazing out at the horizon. Close by her was a short flight of wooden steps that led down to the landing stage where her small boat was tied up. It was a centerboard sloop, slim and graceful.

He went over to her.

"Hello, Elaine."

She turned and her long blond hair swung and flashed in the sun. She smiled at him with an eager, welcoming smile.

"Bruce."

"Called your home and your father said you were down here."

She laughed softly, yet he noted that deep in her gray eyes was a pain. A pain of loss that never seemed to leave them.

"Just playing around with the carburetor. Just for the hell of it."

"And how is it?"

"Okay. I hope it's okay."

"What is it? A four-horsepower?"

She nodded.

"Uh-huh. I've been thinking of getting a six. But a four is better for my kind of a boat."

"I guess it is."

"I'm going to take her out and see how she works. Want to come along?"

"Okay."

"Maybe out to the Point and back. How does that hit you?"

"Good enough, Elaine."

She got up, a small, slight girl in T-shirt and jeans and light blue sneakers. He thought of Ed standing tall against her. Tall and lithe with the body of a distance runner. A glimmering white body with the gray smoke swirling about it.

He had dreamed again of Ed and Raymond running around the cinder track of the athletic field. Running so effortlessly, side by side. He had dreamed last night after the bitter argument with his father. And this time he tried so hard to catch up to them, so very hard. Ran till his breath came in agonized gasps and his heart seemed ready to burst from his body. He called out to them, again and again, and he seemed to be gaining on them, almost to be able to reach out to touch Ed's hand when the dream exploded in a spectrum of colored lights. The lights flashed out and all became black and endless. He awoke. Cold and sweating and trembling violently. His father standing over him and asking, Bruce, Bruce, what is it? What's wrong? What is it?

His mother's form behind him, pale in the doorway.

And he knew that he must have been shouting desperately to Ed and Raymond, begging them to stop and wait for him, shouting loud enough to wake his parents from their sleep.

He said nothing to his father, just held out his hand to him and his father took it gently and after a while, the two of them, his father and his mother, silently left the room.

Soon he fell asleep again, but this time it was a dreamless sleep.

In the morning, when he woke to a cold, drizzling rain, he decided that he must speak to Elaine. Speak to her before it was too late.

Elaine got into the boat first, the sun bright and dazzling behind her, giving her hair a golden aureole. She stood there, held her hand out to him, and helped him to get in and sit down.

"I can make it easy," he protested.

She carefully lay his cane at his side.

"It's my ship. I don't want anybody falling overboard."

They both laughed. She seemed awfully glad to see him. She patted him and bent over and started the outboard going.

He leaned back and let the sun play over him as she guided the little sloop out from the dock and threaded it through the maze of anchored boats and out and free onto the glistening waters of the Sound.

Glistening and rippling with flashes of white gold.

He put his hand over his eyes, shading them, and he felt warm and good. All was so serene and so far away from bleak reality.

"How does it sound to you, Bruce?"

He listened to the even throb of the motor.

"Okay. What was wrong with it?"

She shrugged.

"Nothing, really. Like I said, I just wanted to fiddle around with it. Tune it a little finer. Just for the hell of doing something."

"In the rain?"

"Uh-huh."

And this time she smiled sadly at him and turned away. They didn't speak to each other again for a long while. He closed his eyes and listened to the soothing sound of the motor and felt the warmth of the healing sun.

Finally, he opened his eyes, sighed gently, and sat up.

"Elaine," he said.

"Yes?"

They were now far out from the dock. And to the left of him he could see the sweep of the esplanade and the tiny benches spaced upon it.

It made him think of the night he sat there and the shadowy figure coming out of the darkness and relentlessly following him.

The mad, low laughter.

It made him see again the haggard face of Reverend Dunn and the glowing cat eyes of the man.

The long bony finger raised high.

"Elaine, I came down to talk to you," he said.

"And?"

He looked directly at her.

"It's about Ed."

She flinched and her lips quivered.

"I . . . I wish you wouldn't, Bruce."

The sea breeze was blowing her hair wild and she reached down and picked up a faded gray cap and put it on her head. It made her look younger and very vulnerable.

Like a very handsome kid, he thought.

"I've got to," he said.

"But why, Bruce?"

He didn't answer, just leaned back and gazed ahead at the sun-filled horizon and the blue water, rippling, rippling, with a low, murmurous song.

"Let it be, Bruce. Please."

It was like hitting a young kid, he thought. I'll try again. A little later. But I must try again.

They came to the Point, a spit of land that curved out and into the broad channel of the Sound. It was green with small trees that straggled to the water's edge. She turned the boat in toward a stand of swaying poplars and then shut the motor off and let the boat drift along. He watched her take out a pack of cigarettes and light one and he wanted to cry out to her not to smoke. He didn't want to see Ed's face again.

She had cupped her small hands away from the breeze, the flame glowed, she puffed and then tossed away the burned matchstick and looked up at him.

Her lips tightened and her small, delicate jaw became firm.

"If you've got to speak then I guess you've got to," she said in a low, metallic voice.

The blue smoke curled up between them and then was lost in the sun.

"It's about Ed's death. The way he died."

"I know the way he died," she said.

He shook his head.

"You don't, Elaine."

Now she turned and stared at him.

"What do you mean?"

"It wasn't what Dan Warner and the fire department say it was."

She took off her cap and swung her hair loose and he could see her hands trembling and the cap almost falling from their grip.

"Bruce, I don't sleep nights," she said.

"I don't either."

"Then let it alone. Please."

He shook his head grimly.

"I can't, Elaine. I just can't."

"Why?"

"Because I've got to think of you. Of your safety."

"My . . . what?"

"And of mine."

"Bruce, what are you talking about?"

"It's true, Elaine."

She sat still and rigid, her face pale and drawn. The cigarette burned her fingers and she dropped it with a short, sharp cry. But she still sat there staring at him. He bent forward, picked up the glowing cigarette, and threw it overboard. His eyes looked up and along the narrow stretch of water to the sandy shore and he thought he saw a figure moving swiftly behind the swaying poplar trees. Then it was gone.

He turned back to her.

"Elaine, Ed was killed. And whoever did it is out to kill you . . . and me."

Her eyes widened.

"Bruce, you're saying crazy things."

"You must believe me."

"No. No. Something has gone wrong with you, Bruce."

"Elaine."

"Haywire."

The word set him off.

"God damn it, Elaine, what about Reverend Dunn?" he asked sharply.

She looked at him bewilderedly.

"Reverend . . . Dunn?"

"Yes. Yes."

"What about him?"

"Don't you know?"

"Know what?"

"Didn't Ed tell you of his phone call?"

She shook her head.

"No. What phone call?"

111

His voice became harsh.

"Elaine, he called Ed and he threatened him. He . . ."

Bruce stopped speaking, for he saw a terrified look come into her eyes. And he knew that she was terrified of him.

"Bruce," she said and her voice almost broke. "Ed never said a word about a phone call. Or a threat to his life."

"He was threatened."

"No. Ed would surely have told me. He would have talked it over with me."

"You're lying."

"Bruce."

"You are."

"Bruce, stop it. You're scaring me."

But he went on relentlessly.

"Elaine, are you keeping anything from me?"

"Why should I?"

"I don't know."

"Why should I?" she said in a low, trembling voice.

He leaned forward to her, his face intense.

"Reverend Dunn never called you?"

"Called me? Me?"

His face became distorted.

"Yes. Yes. You."

"Bruce, for God's sake . . ."

He caught her hand and held it tight.

"Tell me the truth.'

"I am telling you the truth."

He shook his head fiercely.

"You're scared and you're lying."

She tried to struggle free from his grasp.

"Bruce, let me go. You're hurting me."

He held her tight.

"You're lying. He must have called you. You were in

112

the car with us. That damned car of death. You were in it with us. I'm sure he called you."

"No, Bruce."

"Why don't you tell me what he said to you?" His voice rose and echoed over the still water. "Why haven't you done something about it? Why, Elaine?"

But she began to cry.

"Bruce, Bruce, please stop it. You're scaring me so. Please. Your face is so wild and brutal. It doesn't seem to belong to you. Your face."

Her last words were whispered.

"My face?"

He slowly released her hand and turned away from her. A fearful look had come into his eyes.

His fingers touched the scars, the tiny scars, and then fell away from them.

"Elaine," he said and his voice was hoarse but gentle.

"Please."

"I'm only trying to help you. To save you."

He had turned back to her and she looked up at him and trembled.

"No. No."

She began to sob.

"Elaine."

He put his hand out to touch her hair and stroke it. But she moved away from him and huddled in a corner of the boat.

Small and slight and heart-rending.

And he remembered her sitting in the chapel, her whole body shaking with her weeping.

What have I done? he asked himself frantically.

He waited till her sobbing ceased.

"Let's get out of here," he said quietly.

She started up the motor again without glancing once to him. They didn't speak to each other all the way back to the dock. When he got out of the boat he paused and looked down at her.

"Your father wanted me to remind you that you're going to your aunt's at six."

"Six?"

"And that you should be home an hour before."

"That means five," she said in a dull voice.

"Five," he repeated mechanically.

Their eyes met and he turned and left her.

"Five," she murmured.

His footsteps faded away and the afternoon silence came in again.

She sat there a long time in the boat. Then she bent over and started up the motor.

She put on the faded gray cap and headed out for the open water. Soon the savage sun blotted out the small figure in the small boat.

19

It was six-thirty that evening when the phone rang. He picked it up.

"Hello?"

"Bruce?"

It was Elaine's father.

"Yes, Mr. Ross."

"Did you see Elaine today?"

"Yes."

"Did you give her my message?"

"About being home at five?"

"That's right. Did you?"

"Yes, Mr. Ross. I told her."

"Are you sure, Bruce?"

"Why? What's wrong?"

"Well, I'm down at the dock and she's not here and the boat's not here."

Bruce felt a chill go through him.

"I'm sure she's still out on the water, Mr. Ross."

"I know she is." Mr. Ross said impatiently. "I know that. But why isn't she back? It's not like her. Not like her at all."

"She'll show up soon."

"Were you out with her today?"

"Yes."

"Out long?"

Bruce hesitated and then spoke.

"We went to the Point and then turned back."

"What time did you leave her, Bruce?"

"About three or so. She was still sitting in the boat. I guess she decided to go out again. It was such a beautiful day."

He thought of what had happened on the boat. How he had frightened her and left her despondent and fearful.

Then he heard the man's voice.

"Yes. It was a fine day. Maybe she decided to go far out and do some swimming. She had her suit on underneath when she left the house."

"It could be that she went back to the Point to walk around there," Bruce said.

"The Point?"

"Yes. She used to go there with Ed a lot."

"Oh. I didn't know that."

"She probably went there."

"Yes. That's possible. And she just lost track of time."

"That's probably it."

But he knew in his heart that something had gone wrong.

"Well, thanks, Bruce."

"I'm sure she'll turn up soon, Mr. Ross."

"I know. It's just that . . ."

And his voice trailed off into silence.

"Mr. Ross," Bruce said.

"Yes?"

"Do you mind if I come down to the dock and wait around with you?"

"I'd appreciate it, Bruce."

"I'll be there in about fifteen minutes."

116

"Okay, Bruce."

"Maybe by that time she'll be back."

"Sure hope so. I'm starting to get anxious, Bruce."

"She'll show up."

"Good-bye, Bruce."

"Good-bye, Mr. Ross."

He put down the phone slowly. Then he got up and picked up his cane and went out of the house.

As he walked his way to the dock, through the file of trees, he felt that someone was following him. But each time he turned and looked there was no one there.

Only the shadows of the trees, long and angular on the sidewalk.

20

It was while they were standing there and the day was starting to darken in the east that they saw a small boat coming in to them. The figure in the boat was small and indistinct.

"It's Elaine," Mr. Ross said in a desperate pleading voice.

"Yes. It looks like her." Bruce murmured hopefully.

"It's Elaine." Mr. Ross shouted.

But as the boat came closer they saw that it was not Elaine. It was Oliver Warner coming in from fishing out in the channel. The dying sun flashed off his black rods and the silver bodies of the fish lying on the floor of his boat.

As he came closer he started to veer to another slip and Mr. Ross called out to him and waved his hand again and again.

"Oliver. Oliver Warner."

Oliver waved back.

"Come this way. I want to talk to you."

Oliver nodded and headed his boat into their slip. Bruce stood there at the side of Mr. Ross, silently watching the small gleaming boat come closer, closer, the outboard motor throbbing evenly in the clear evening air and then suddenly being cut off and the stillness rushing in.

And all the time he thought of Elaine sitting in the corner of her boat, sitting huddled, and sobbing.

He bent his head and closed his eyes in pain.

Oliver called out.

"What is it, Mr. Ross?"

Oliver's face and arms were red from the sun.

"Did you see Elaine out there?"

"Elaine?"

And for an instant he didn't seem to know who Elaine was. He looked blankly at them.

"My daughter, Oliver. My daughter."

Oliver shook his head and stood up, the fading sun behind him, outlining his tall figure.

"No, Mr. Ross."

"No sign of her at all?"

A look of concern came over Oliver's face.

"Why? What's wrong?"

And Bruce remembered that he had asked the same question when Mr. Ross phoned him. Using the very same words.

"She was supposed to be back at five. It's close to eight now."

"Were you anywhere near the Point?" Bruce asked.

Oliver looked up at Bruce and for an instant, a flashing instant, Bruce thought he could see a glint of wild amusement in Oliver's eyes. And he said to himself, What in the hell does Oliver see that's funny in this?

Mr. Ross was almost out of his head with worry.

"No, Bruce," Oliver said and the look of concern was back in his eyes.

"Didn't see her," Mr. Ross muttered and turned away from them.

"I used to see her swimming far out," Oliver said.

"A lot of times. She always likes to swim out there. Very few boats around. And she's a top swimmer. Probably the best around here. I didn't see her this time."

But Mr. Ross didn't seem to be listening to him. He just stood there, a stocky man with a bowed head.

"She could be out at the Point," Bruce said.

Oliver nodded thoughtfully.

"Could be. She'd go out there with Ed a lot."

"I know."

"We ought to take a look."

"I think it's worth it."

"Mr. Ross," Oliver said.

The man turned questioningly.

"Yes?"

"Why don't you and Bruce get into my boat," Oliver said gently. "We'll go out to the Point and look around there before it gets too dark."

"The Point?"

"It's a good idea," Bruce said.

The man looked at Bruce and there was no hope in him.

"All right," he said.

21

It was just as darkness fell that the little sloop was found drifting off the Point. Oliver was the first to sight it.

"That looks like her boat," he called out sharply.

"Yes," Bruce said.

Her father stood up.

"Elaine!" he shouted. "Elaine!"

There was no answer.

"Elaine!" Bruce called and there was a break in his voice, and he didn't know why it was there.

"We'll get closer," Oliver said.

He revved up the motor and soon they were almost upon the sloop. They could see that there was no one in it.

"Where is she?"

They pulled up side to side and Mr. Ross was the first to jump into the boat. He began to search frantically about it.

From where Bruce stood he could see the neat pile of clothing—the T-shirt, the jeans, and the sneakers.

"She went swimming," Oliver said.

"But . . ."

Bruce didn't say any more. The boat was drifting, he

thought. She would never do that. Go swimming and let it drift this way.

That was not how she did things. Not Elaine.

And suddenly he heard a cry.

"Elaine."

Mr. Ross was standing up in the sloop and shouting to the world around him. The empty, darkening world.

"Elaine! Elaine! Elaine!"

And Bruce, listening to the father's cry, thought his own heart would break.

22

The search went on all through the night. Voices sounded against the darkness and huge arc lights played over the water. Morning came. The Coast Guard had come out and divers had gone down time and time again looking for the body of Elaine Ross. Bruce went home and slept a few restless hours and then Oliver picked him up and they drove down to the dock and sailed out in Oliver's boat again.

"Let's hope they've found her," Oliver said.

"Found her alive."

Oliver looked calmly at him.

"That's what I meant."

Ahead of them was a wide cluster of boats. It was just past noon and the sun was high and shining with a fierce light. There was little breeze. The water was blue and rippling, and Bruce thought of yesterday and sitting in the little sloop with Elaine and listening to the murmuring song of the water. He saw her again with the gray cap over her long blond hair.

He looked ahead of him to the spaced vessels, gleaming and rocking ever so slightly in the sun.

It's a regatta, he said to himself. The boats are gathered together for the annual regatta. Boats of all shapes and sizes. Come from different communities. All gathered together and everything is so white and joyous and flashing.

Elaine is alive.

Alive.

And soon she'll stand up in her little centerboard sloop, wave her hand, and lead all the other vessels out, far, far out toward the shining horizon.

He heard Oliver's voice.

"Anything doing?"

They had come close to one of the boats and a figure standing on its white deck turned and gazed down at them.

"Nothing," the figure said.

"No sign of Elaine?"

"None. She's down in the bottom somewhere around here. They'll find her sooner or later."

And the figure turned away from them.

"That's one of her uncles," Oliver said.

His face was white and drawn.

"He's trying to be hard and blunt about it," Bruce said.

"But he's hurting bad," Oliver said.

"We all are."

"I guess we are," Oliver murmured.

They saw a diver come out of the water, smooth and black and wet, lift himself over the bow of a boat, and disappear from sight.

"Zero," Oliver said.

"Looks like it."

"And it's going to be zero all day."

"Why do you say that?"

"How else could it be? It's tough to find a body in this depth of water."

Bruce nodded slowly.

"It is."

"And who knows where she went down? Was swimming and got a stomach cramp and went down. That's the only way it happens with a strong swimmer. Who knows where? Do you? Have you any idea?"

"Then you think she's dead," Bruce said.

Oliver turned to him and there was a bleak look in his eyes. He had pushed back his hair with the same motion that Raymond always used.

"Yes, Bruce," he said in a flat, metallic voice. "And so do you. And everybody else."

"Maybe she's on the Point. Walking around somewhere. Maybe she's . . ."

He stopped speaking.

"You're not making sense," Oliver said.

Bruce gazed at him and sighed low.

"I'm not."

"You're hoping. And in this life hopes don't count for much. Most times they add up to nothing. Haven't you found that out yet?"

"I guess I have, Oliver."

Oliver grunted.

"Walking around the Point. You weren't serious about that, were you?"

Bruce flushed.

"I was hoping. A crazy hope."

"It was."

"Let's forget it," Bruce said quietly.

Oliver smiled tolerantly.

"Sure. But just to lock it up. They've been searching the Point for hours, Bruce. My old man's been out there with a search party and they've come up blank. Nothing. Told me so just before I left home to pick you up."

"You told him you were going to pick me up?"

"That's right."

And Bruce thought of Dan Warner telling Bruce never to come to his office again.

"Your father say anything else?" Bruce asked.

Oliver shook his head.

"That was it. He doesn't talk much these days."

"I had a run-in with him at his office," Bruce said.

Oliver's eyes narrowed.

"That's easy to do. He's running a short fuse these days. Has lots of run-ins. But don't tell me about yours."

"I'd like to, Oliver."

"I'm not interested."

"But . . ."

Oliver shook his head grimly.

"No, Bruce. Let it lie."

"Okay, Oliver," Bruce said in a low voice. "Okay."

"The past is the past. Let it alone. Let it die in peace."

Oliver started up the motor again.

"Where are we going?" Bruce asked.

Oliver waved his hand in disgust.

"No sense in our sticking around here any longer. We'll try the other side of the Point. Maybe we'll come up with something."

He swung the boat wide to make a sweep around the search area.

"But that would be a helluva long way for her to swim, Oliver."

Oliver shrugged.

"I know."

"The boat was found drifting here."

Oliver smiled coldly at him.

"You're forgetting that I was the one who found it."

"I know that. I'm just trying to . . ."

Oliver cut in softly.

"We've got to try everything, Bruce. They've come

up dry on this side of the Point. Let's see what's doing along the other side."

"Okay," Bruce muttered.

Oliver leaned back and smiled gently at Bruce.

"Let me have my way."

"I am."

"Good."

They were now clear of the boats and ahead of them was the spread of blue water and the cloudless sky shimmering above it.

Oliver broke the silence.

"You don't like to lose, do you, Bruce?"

"What?"

"But sometimes we all lose. All of us. Isn't that what life is about?"

Bruce didn't speak.

"Raymond's death made a cynic out of me. You'll have to put up with it. The world will have to put up with it. And if they can't, tough on them."

I can't read you, Oliver, Bruce thought. I just can't read you.

Oliver answered as if reading Bruce's thoughts.

"Forgive me, Bruce, I'm in a strange mood today."

"It's nothing," Bruce said.

"That's what it is. Nothing. Life. Death. Nothing. Who cares if they find Elaine or not? It's all nothing. *Nada. Nada.* And again *nada.* Do you ever read Hemingway? You ought to. He's a fine writer. You'll find *nada, nada, nada,* in one of his fine stories. You should read Hemingway, Bruce."

And then he was silent.

They rounded the Point and Oliver headed the boat in toward the file of trees and the shallower water. He cut the motor down when they came closer to the sandy strip of beach and then they went slowly along it and all the time neither said a word. A pall seemed to have settled over them. Oliver sat in the stern, straight and rigid, his eyes staring ahead.

A flock of birds, small and gray, flew up from the shore and over them and Bruce watched them become distant specks in the sky and he thought of Ed and the airplane that flew over them as they sat in the darkening athletic field and the silver plane becoming a speck and finally vanishing.

He felt that he must speak.

"I have a strange, strange feeling about all this," he said.

"What do you mean?"

Bruce looked squarely at him.

"It's about the Car of Death."

Oliver paled and trembled slightly.

"What are you talking about?" he asked harshly.

"The car that Raymond and I and Ed and Elaine rode in. Your car. I've come to call it the Car of Death, Oliver."

"Cut it, Bruce. I don't want to hear another word."

Bruce leaned forward intensely.

"But you must. There's Reverend Dunn. He called Ed before his death. He called me. He talked to me. He followed me. And I'm sure he's threatened Elaine."

Oliver cut off the motor with a sharp motion. The boat drifted closer to the shore. His face was tight and drawn.

"I don't want you to go on, Bruce."

"I have to."

"Damnit, I asked you in the hospital to lay off. I asked you before to let the past go. Let it go, Bruce." His voice rose. "God damn you, let it go!"

But Bruce went on.

"Your father won't look for Reverend Dunn. He says he's dead."

"Bruce."

"But Reverend Dunn is alive. He's out to kill me, too. I know it. Oliver, I tell you something has happened to Elaine. I know it. I can feel it in my bones. I'm telling you she was killed."

Oliver rose to his full height.

"Another word and I'll throw you out of the boat, cane and all, and let you drown. I don't want to hear any more."

Bruce stared up at him.

"Throw you out and let you drown, for all I care."

"I bet you would, Oliver."

"Damn right I would."

Bruce looked fully at him.

"Okay," he said. "I'm through speaking."

Oliver slowly sat down. He put his hand to his brow and drew it away wet with perspiration.

He sat there, looking dully at the glistening palm. His chest heaved and his breath was short.

"I didn't mean to upset you this way," Bruce said.

"Sure," Oliver muttered, not looking up.

"You're running a short fuse. Just like your father."

Oliver looked up and his face became stony like Dan Warner's. The eyes were cold and metallic.

"Like my father," he said.

He leaned forward abruptly and started the motor again. This time he shot it up to top speed and the boat leaped forward and high and then slapped down and roared along the water, stirring up little, angry waves.

His hair blew in the breeze.

"Like my father," he shouted. "Like Police Chief Daniel Warner. Greatest police officer in the United States. Best father. Best husband. All-around success. Daniel H. Warner, I salute you."

He put his right hand to his forehead in a smart

salute and then dropped it to his side. He slouched down and abruptly cut the motor low and the boat crept along, its motor purring.

Bruce thought of the purring of a cat and of the cat eyes of Reverend Dunn. Hazel, glowing, and impenetrable.

Oliver turned to Bruce and Bruce was startled to see tears streaming down his face.

"I'm sorry, Bruce," he said. "I loved Raymond so much. So very much."

"Yes," Bruce whispered.

"I go crazy when I think about him dead. My mind blows out. You understand? You do, Bruce? Don't you?"

"Yes," Bruce whispered again.

Oliver wiped the tears from his face. When he spoke again his voice was low and controlled.

"I'll talk to my father about Reverend Dunn. You'll tell me more. When I feel up to it. Okay?"

And Bruce was about to answer him when he saw the white body of Elaine Ross floating near the shore.

He could only point to it.

He could not speak.

23

Death by drowning. The body being slowly drawn to shore by the currents. Where Elaine Ross went down was hard to determine.

A stomach cramp.

Could not get back to the boat in time and sank to her death. The boat slowly drifting away on a calm sea until it was found.

But nobody can really explain why the boat was drifting, Bruce thought as he sat in the shadowed chapel. Somebody pulled up the anchor and let the boat drift. That's the only way it could have happened.

But she must have noticed it. And then what did she do about it?

She didn't drown.

Somebody made her drown.

It had to be that way. It had to.

But who would believe me? Who?

No one.

"May her soul rest in peace."

And he suddenly realized that the service was over. He hadn't heard a word of it. He glanced about him, not seeing anybody, all a blur to him, and he made his way outside into the sun.

He watched the people come out and he moved farther away from them and stood alone and cold in the blazing sun.

"Bruce Kendall?"

He turned and saw the pale face of Mr. Carlson, the former owner of the tavern.

"Yes?"

The man came closer to him and Bruce felt a wild impulse to turn and run. This was the last man on earth he wanted to see now. It brought back the night of the crash so vividly and so painfully to him.

"It's terrible, isn't it?" Carlson said in a low, weak voice.

The man had lost weight. His dark suit hung on him and the collar of his white shirt was loose around the neck. Bruce gazing at Carlson realized with a deep pang how much he must have suffered and lost.

"It is," Bruce murmured.

"A young, sweet girl. Innocent."

"Yes."

"I understand that she was a wonderful student. Wanted to become a doctor."

A veterinarian," Bruce said. "She loved animals."

Carlson shook his head mournfully.

"Such a waste of life. Such a tragic waste."

"Yes."

And he thought how much he had dreaded seeing Carlson. Facing his hatred. But now all he could see before him was a broken and sympathetic human being.

Carlson had lost everything.

"Mr. Carlson," he said.

"Yes, Bruce?"

"I know what has happened to you since the accident. How you lost your place."

"I lost it," the man said sadly.

"I've been wanting to come to tell you how sorry I am about it."

The man shrugged hopelessly.

"It's gone. Gone forever. I've nothing left."

"I remember how hard you tried to get us to leave. And how badly I treated you then. Could you ever forgive me?"

"Of course, Bruce. I was somewhat to blame, too. I guess I brought it all on myself."

"It was a bad night," Bruce said and turned away from him as he spoke, not wanting to see the pain in the man's face. It had become unbearable to him.

And then he heard Carlson say, "You're the only one left from the car. Aren't you?"

He turned back to Carlson and for an instant he thought he could see a gleam of triumph in the man's sunken eyes.

"Yes," Bruce said. "The only one."

The gleam was gone and silence came in.

They stood there under the sun with the people moving about them. There seemed to be nothing more to say, yet Carlson remained at his side.

Like a gray conscience.

And then he heard a voice, low and curt.

"Carlson."

They both turned and saw Dan Warner coming up to them.

"Yes?"

"I thought I told you to stay away from Kendall."

Carlson trembled.

"I know, Dan. But I . . . I . . ."

He stopped speaking and Bruce could feel the fear that was overwhelming the man. It made Bruce angry at Warner.

135

"He wasn't bothering me, Mr. Warner," Bruce said. "We were just standing here and talking to each other about Elaine."

"That's all it was, Dan."

"He's right," Bruce said.

Warner whirled upon Bruce.

"Just shut up and let me handle this," he said harshly.

Bruce paled and tensed.

"All right," he said quietly, but inside he was seething.

Warner turned back to Carlson and Bruce could see the hatred that filled Dan Warner. A blazing hatred of the tavern owner.

Warner's big right hand rested on the handle of his police revolver. He doesn't realize it's there, Bruce thought. How much he wants to draw the gun from its holster and fire it again and again into Carlson's head.

I know that's how he feels at this moment.

Capable of murder.

It is so clear.

"I thought you're leaving town for good," Warner said.

"Tomorrow," Carlson said.

"That's not too soon for me. You never should have come to this community in the first place. The day you came here you brought a curse."

Carlson seemed to stiffen.

"Let me alone, will you," he said in a bitter voice.

"Why should I?"

"Stop hounding me."

"I'll hound you till you are out of this town for good."

"I'll go when I'm ready."

"All right. That's enough of your lip. Shut up."

"I'll speak as much as I want."

Warner moved closer to Carlson.

"Now look," he said grimly. "I don't want ever to see the two of you together again." He turned to Bruce. "That means you also, Bruce."

"If that's how you want it," Bruce said.

"That's how I want it."

He turned back to Carlson.

"Start moving, Carlson."

The man remained in his spot.

"I can stay where I want."

"I said, keep moving."

He put his hand to Carlson's shoulder and the man flung it away. A flame leaped into his sunken eyes. His slack face became tight with fury.

"Four little Indians in a car. And then there were none," he shouted, his voice echoing out over the smooth green lawn and making people stop speaking and stand still.

Warner stepped back from him.

"What the hell do you mean by that?"

Carlson bent forward to him. His voice now came out in a fierce whisper.

"You figure it out, Mr. Policeman." He turned sharply to Bruce. "You too, Mr. Kendall."

And then Carlson walked away from them.

24

Four little Indians riding in a car. And then there were none. He was thinking of that as he walked from the grave to the cortege of limousines. He was walking alone and apart from the others when he heard the voice.

"Bruce."

It was low and soft and appealing.

"Marian."

She looked so much like Elaine and yet she was taller and had a lithe figure. But the hair was blond and the features small and the eyes gray. And he felt a quivering in his heart as he stood there gazing at her.

"Why don't you ever see me anymore?"

He stood there, not answering her.

"What have I done, Bruce? We were always such good friends."

"You've done nothing, Marian," he said.

He moved under the shade of a tree and the sunlight flickered through the leaves and down onto them.

"Then what is it?"

"It's so hard to explain, Marian," he said.

"But don't you think I deserve something? Some words?"

He nodded.

"Yes."

"Couldn't you try to tell me?"

He looked away from her and he saw standing under another tree, far off, the black figure. He knew it was Reverend Dunn.

He trembled.

"Bruce. Bruce, what's wrong?"

"It's nothing, Marian. Nothing. I . . . I just thought of something unpleasant. That's all."

"What was it?"

He shook his head.

"Let's forget it."

She kept looking at him, a bewildered, hurt expression in her eyes and he wanted to put his arm around her and draw her to him, but he stood silent and motionless, leaning forward on his cane.

"Bruce, what have I done?" she asked. "What?"

"Marian, it's me," he said gently. "I'm the one who's done the wrong to you. I know it. And yet there's not a thing I can do about it."

She shook her head bewilderedly.

"I don't understand you."

"Marian, I don't understand myself. I . . . this is not the time to talk about it. Not after what happened to Elaine. It's not the time. It's not the place."

"I know, Bruce."

The tears welled into her eyes and she turned away from him, her head bowed. And he thought of Elaine sitting huddled in the boat, weeping.

The words pushed out of him.

"I don't know what it was," he said. "Maybe it was the face. This lousy new face. Maybe that. Maybe . . . the cane . . . the . . . I don't know, Marian. Maybe it was the damned sense of guilt."

140

She turned sharply to him.

"Guilt?"

He slowly nodded his head.

"Yes."

"But why? For what?"

"For what?"

"Yes, Bruce. Yes. What are you guilty of? What are you saying?"

And he was on the verge of telling her what really had happened in the car that fatal night. But his eyes caught the sight of the figure under the tree. And the fear and dismay that rose in him cut off all speech.

She came close to him.

"Bruce, what guilt?"

"Please, Marian," he said.

But she went on.

"Tell me. Please."

He shook his head.

"No."

He saw the figure and this time a ray of sunlight slanted down full upon it, making its blackness flash and shimmer.

He trembled and moved back from her.

"Let's get out of here," he said.

"Why?"

"Marian, I . . ."

She put her hand tenderly on him.

"Bruce, what guilt? Is it that Raymond died and you lived? Is that it, Bruce?"

"Maybe that," he said.

Her hand stroked his hair.

"But you had nothing to do with it."

"Nothing?"

She looked fully at him, her eyes large.

"That was in the hands of God."

He glanced to the dark figure and suddenly he understood the Reverend Dunn. Understood him thoroughly.

"And God has sent down an executioner," he said.

"What?"

"That's what it is."

Her lips had fallen open, but she did not speak.

"Yes, Marian," he said wildly. "An executioner. And who's to stand in the way of God's executioner? Who? Tell me."

"Bruce," she whispered, her face pale.

"Tell me. Tell me, Marian. Who?"

"Bruce, you're speaking so strangely. You're scaring me."

He thought of Elaine saying the same words to him.

"Oh, leave me alone," he said bitterly. "Leave me to my punishment."

He turned and walked away from her. As he did, the dark figure slid away from the tree and vanished in the sunlight.

25

The vault box was open. A hand descended slowly and picked up the white sheet of paper that was in the box. Picked it up, held it in the dim light, and slowly the two words were read aloud in the privacy of the vault booth.

"By earth."

The executioner smiled.

"The third shall die by earth."

The left hand closed into a fist. Now the hand flew open and a spray of fine dark earth fell into the box, as into a grave.

"By earth. And then it will all be over."

The paper was put back into the metal box and the box returned to the shelf of the vault.

"Have a good day," the guard said.

"I will."

The executioner turned and smiled to the guard.

"Is not vengeance mine, saith the Lord?"

26

He was sitting in the kitchen drinking coffee and gazing out the window at the slow oncoming night when his father came into the room, paused at the threshold, went over to the stove, poured himself coffee, and sat down on the other side of the table.

The rest of the house was silent.

"Bruce."

Bruce looked over to him.

"Well?"

"Think we can speak to each other a little?"

"It all depends."

"On what we speak about?"

"Yes."

His father drank a little coffee and set the cup down.

"Mom and I are going away."

Bruce felt a trembling start within him. He did his best to control it.

"When?"

"In a few days."

"Anything urgent?"

His father shook his head.

"We figure on going to the Coast for a little vacation. Two weeks or so."

Bruce thought of himself alone in the house and he didn't speak. He turned away from his father and looked out the window at the darkening sky. Then he focused on the leaves of the small, lean poplar tree that stood in the yard. The dying sun flecked them with touches of fire.

He heard his father's voice. It was gentle.

"We thought we'd like you to come along with us, Bruce."

"Oh."

"We'll have a good time together. We have in the past."

"I guess we did," Bruce said.

His father looked appealingly over to him.

"Well, Bruce?"

"You're not really going for yourselves," Bruce said.

His father flushed.

"Of course we are, Bruce. And we want you along."

Bruce shook his head.

"You want me to get away from here. Isn't that it?"

"But . . ."

"Isn't it?"

His father sighed and slowly nodded.

"Yes, Bruce. It is."

"Why?"

His father gazed down to his cup and then played with the shining rim a while. His finger ran around the rim, again and again.

Slowly. Ever so slowly.

"You're not looking so well, son," he said.

"Not looking too well and not acting too well," Bruce muttered.

They were silent. A soft evening breeze rustled the leaves of the poplar tree and then all was quiet again.

"Do I still have nightmares that wake you up?" Bruce asked gently.

"You should get away for a rest, Bruce."

"Do I?"

"Why do you want to know?"

"Just curious."

His father hesitated and put the cup down delicately. It sat there on the table, small, white, and gleaming.

"Last night in your sleep. You . . . You . . . It was toward morning. Just before sunlight. Yes, just before sunlight."

And his father stopped speaking.

"What happened?"

"You started to sob."

Bruce stared at him.

"Toward morning?"

"Yes."

"And?"

"You cried out, Don't kill me, I don't want to die."

"You heard me?"

"Yes."

"Mom, too?"

His father nodded yes. The breeze came up again and this time he saw it rustle the soft fine hairs of his father's head.

"Bruce," his father said.

"Well?"

"Bruce, what is it? What's . . . ?"

"It's no use talking about it," Bruce cut in sharply.

"We know of Ed and Elaine. We know that you feel they were . . ."

"Murdered," Bruce cut in quietly.

"Bruce."

"Oh, what's the use?" Bruce said bitterly. "You still think what you think, and I think what I think. And that's how the damned thing is."

"Dan Warner and all the rest say that the deaths were due to . . ."

147

"To hell with Dan Warner," Bruce said.

"He's been doing his best to find out the truth. He's an excellent police officer. His record is one of the best."

"Oh, to hell with all that crap. Stop it."

His father took off his glasses and looked at them slowly, deliberately, his face white with anger and pain, and then he put the gold-rimmed glasses on again.

"Bruce, I didn't come in here to upset you. To make things worse than they are. I came in here to talk to you. To . . ."

"Well, goddamnit, it always ends up that way, doesn't it? Me shouting at you and you shouting at me."

"Yes," his father said.

Bruce looked across to the man and he felt welling up within him a great love and compassion.

And yet when he spoke it was with bitterness.

"When I'm dead you'll know I was right."

His father stood up.

"Bruce."

Bruce waved his hand at him.

"You'll see who was right."

"Bruce, damnit, don't speak that way. You won't die. Please don't say such things. Get that out of your head."

"Sure."

"I ask you, please don't think such thoughts."

"I'll try not to," Bruce said sarcastically.

He saw how much he was hurting his father.

"All right," Bruce said wearily. "I'll go with you. Make the reservations."

His father looked at him and Bruce thought he was about to cry.

"You will?"

"Yes," Bruce said softly. "I'll go."

"We'll have a good time, Bruce. Believe me, we will."

"Okay, Dad. We will."

He watched his father go out of the room and he sat down again and gazed out of the window.

He saw the tree standing stark and silent. The leaves were losing the touches of fire and were turning black.

I'll never make that trip, he thought. I'll be dead before it.

27

He was looking at his face in the mirror and comparing it with the face on some photographs that were taken more than a year ago, looking at his face in the pictures and then at the small etched scars in the mirrored face, looking and feeling bleak and hopeless, when the phone rang.

The clear sound filled the room, chilling it. He let the phone ring and then it stopped. After a brief pause, it started again.

He kept listening to the insistent ringing.

Finally, he picked up the black receiver.

"Hello?"

"Bruce?"

He breathed a sigh of relief.

"Hello, Oliver," he said.

"You alone?"

"Yes."

"Thought so. Most everybody is alone these days."

"Folks are out shopping. Buying some last things. We're going out to the Coast on a trip. Down around L.A. way."

He suddenly felt himself opened up and eager to talk to Oliver.

"When are you going?"

"Day after tomorrow. And then we go up the Coast highway to San Francisco."

"Sounds great. Wait another month and I'll meet you out there."

"That's when you go back to college?"

"That's right, Bruce. Got an idea. See how you like the Coast and then tell me when you get back."

"And?"

"Later on you can come out and stay with me for a while. I'll show you around and we'll have a good time together."

"Sounds good, Oliver."

"We'll work it out. And we'll get real close to each other. You and I, Bruce."

"Okay with me."

"You were Raymond's best friend. You'll be mine, Bruce."

"I'd like to, Oliver."

And as he said those words the present slid away from him and he thought of himself out on the Coast with Oliver, walking along the tree-lined campus, the sun above them, walking as he used to walk with Raymond, and all the world serene again.

"So think about it, Bruce."

"I will."

"Great stuff, Bruce."

He heard Oliver's warm laugh and it elated him and then suddenly he heard Oliver speak again and this time there was no laughter in the voice.

"Four little Indians in a car."

He was thrust back into the present, the terrifying present.

"What?"

And he said to himself desperately, I can't read you, Oliver. I just can't

152

"My old man told me what Carlson said to the two of you. Four little Indians in a car. At Elaine's funeral."

"Oh," Bruce said.

"Carlson's out of his skull these days, Bruce. Pay no attention to him."

"I know," Bruce murmured.

"He's a weak, broken man. Capable of nothing. A nothing man. Forget him."

"Yes."

"But just the same, what he said kind of set me thinking. Thinking a helluva lot. That's why I called you."

Bruce didn't speak. He was thinking of Carlson.

Then he heard Oliver's voice, soft and easy.

"I've been going over in my mind what you said to me on the boat. When we were out, you and I, searching for Elaine."

And Bruce saw again Oliver's tense white face before him. And heard again the savage, wild words that Oliver spoke then.

Another word and I'll throw you out of the boat, cane and all, and let you drown. I don't want to hear any more.

And he saw Oliver sitting there, the tears streaming down his face.

I loved Raymond so much. So very much.

"Bruce, Bruce, are you there?"

"What?"

"I've been speaking to you and I get no answer."

"I'm sorry, Oliver."

"I've been talking about Reverend William Dunn."

Bruce looked about him and saw the shadows of night begin to come into the room. Outside all was quiet and expectant.

"I know," he said.

"I've been thinking a lot about him, Bruce. And I've been out looking for him."

"You have, Oliver?"

The tree outside the window, the tree in the yard, was silent and still.

"You say he made calls to you and Ed?"

"Yes."

"Kind of weird, threatening calls?"

Bruce nodded.

"He spoke of our sins and of paying for them. He said the wages of sin are death.

He heard Oliver laugh, a low, harsh laugh.

"They are, Bruce. They are. The fellow upstairs sees to it. Doesn't he?"

Bruce didn't answer. He heard Oliver laugh low again.

"That God, that force that rules over everything. He sees to it, doesn't he? He wants blood for blood, doesn't he?"

"I guess he does," Bruce murmured.

But he said to himself, I can't read you, Oliver. I just can't.

"And you say he called Elaine?"

Bruce stirred himself.

"Elaine? Yes, I'm sure of it. Called her and threatened her. I could swear that he did, Oliver."

There was a pause and he saw his face in the mirror and it was white in the shadows.

"You believe that Ed and Elaine were murdered," Oliver said.

"I know it," Bruce said, his voice rising. "I tell you I know it."

"All right. Hold on," Oliver said calmly. "Don't let yourself get worked up. I believe you, Bruce."

"I'm next in line," Bruce said. "He's out to kill me. Like he did the others."

"Nobody's going to kill you, Bruce. So lay off that idea."

"But nobody believes me. Your father just looks at me and . . ."

"Forget him," Oliver cut in. "He'll believe only when you confront him with the facts. He has no imagination. None at all."

"He says he can't find Reverend Dunn. He says he's dead. And yet the man finds me pretty easily. He was at Ed's funeral. He spoke to me. And I saw him at Elaine's funeral."

"Bruce, I believe you and I'm with you all the way. He's around here somewhere."

"I know he is."

"Well, I've got a hunch where we can find him."

Bruce drew in his breath

"You have, Oliver?"

"Yes. I've been doing a lot of driving around Cordell. Cruising around and talking to some people. I've got a good lead."

"Where do you think he is?"

"I'd like to check out that little house just off the road near Carter's farm."

"Nobody's lived there for three years."

"That's just it. I saw a light through the trees. Last night."

"Then somebody is there."

"Somebody sure is, Bruce. Want to come along with me and check it out? We find him, then we call up my old man and have him come down and grill him. Well?"

"Tonight?"

"Time is running out on you, Bruce," Oliver said softly.

Bruce didn't speak. He looked down at his left hand and it was trembling slightly. The hand holding the phone had begun to sweat.

Then he heard Oliver's voice thread through the shadows to him.

"The way I see it, Reverend Dunn looks upon that Car of Death as a Car of Sin. You remember you called it a Car of Death?"

"Yes."

"Well, this weirdo believes that sins must be punished. And the way I see it, he sees himself as God's sacred and chosen executioner."

Bruce trembled and the hand gripping the phone almost dropped it.

"Executioner?"

"Well, how else could he think? Try sitting in his skull, Bruce. You'll come to the same conclusion that I did."

"I have," Bruce said slowly. "Those are the words I said to Marian. I said that he is God's executioner."

"That's the only way he can justify to himself his being a murderer, Bruce."

Bruce was silent.

"Isn't that so?"

"Yes," Bruce said in a low voice.

"Let's find out and then we'll know the truth."

Bruce gazed about him. Soon it will be night, he thought. Dark, enveloping night. And then the words came to him, "Where have you gone, Joe DiMaggio?"

The words and tune of the song.

And then they were gone.

"I'll drop by in fifteen minutes and pick you up, Bruce."

"All right, Raymond," he said.

He heard Oliver gasp.

"Raymond?"

"I . . . I mean Oliver."

He wondered why he had made the mistake. Then he remembered that Raymond always liked to play the

Simon and Garfunkel record of Mrs. Robinson. And to sing the words, "Where have you gone, Joe Di-Maggio?" over and over again.

"It's interesting that you should call me Raymond," he heard Oliver say, and his voice was now placid. "Because it gives me an idea. My father tells me that he gave you Raymond's hat. Bring it along."

"The hat? Why, Oliver?"

"It could prove effective. Just bring it along."

"But . . ."

"Fifteen minutes. So long, Bruce."

There was a click.

"So long, Oliver," Bruce murmured.

He put down the phone and sat there a long time in the gloom. He rose and put on the lamplight and went to the closet. He reached up and searched about the top shelf where he had placed the hat.

He could not find it.

He stood there puzzled and uneasy.

He took a chair and stood on it and rummaged all over the shelf. He got off the chair and knelt and began searching along the floor of the closet. He turned around and scanned the room.

It was gone.

Slowly the chilling thought came to him that someone had come into the house and up to the room and into the closet and taken away the hat.

Raymond's floppy hat.

28

28

"You say he was in the cemetery at Elaine's funeral?"

"Yes, Oliver. I saw him standing by a tree."

"But he didn't come up to you?"

"No. I was talking to Marian. He just stood there, far off, watching me. Then he went away."

"He hasn't phoned you?"

"No."

Oliver nodded and turned to the road again. He lounged back in his seat, his dark hair falling over his white forehead, his long hand loosely holding the wheel.

"Better put on your headlights, Oliver," Bruce said. "It's starting to get dark."

"Sure thing."

Oliver switched on the lights and Bruce could see the ribbon of narrow highway stretching ahead of them.

"Describe the man to me again, Bruce."

"Oh. Lean in a black suit. A white panama hat. Hazel eyes. Cat eyes. High cheekbones. Haggard-looking sort of a man."

"Cat eyes?"

"Yes."

"There's no mercy in cat eyes. Ever notice that?"

"Not when it's caught a mouse."

"Exactly."

"And I'm his mouse," Bruce murmured.

"He hasn't caught you yet, Bruce. And he won't."

Oliver reached over and patted Bruce gently on the shoulder.

"I'm scared, Oliver," Bruce said. "It's as simple as that. Scared and all mixed up."

"Just take it easy."

"I'm scared," Bruce said again.

Oliver smiled gently at him and then they were silent.

They rode along, all was still and vast about them, every now and then a car would pass, and then they would be alone again. Somehow Bruce began to feel that he was sitting in the car with Raymond at the wheel. And that the swiftly oncoming night was the same as the one during the fatal winter and the trees the same, even though now they were thick with summer leaves.

Leaves that flashed in the headlights and then became dark and lost.

He glanced over to Oliver.

"I can't make out what happened to the hat," he said.

Oliver shrugged.

"You'll find it sooner or later."

Bruce shook his head.

"No. Someone came in when the house was empty and took it away."

"That's hard to believe."

"I'm sure that's what happened."

"But why should anyone want the hat?"

"I don't know. What did you want it for, Oliver?"

Oliver smiled.

"No point in going into it now. The hat's gone. The

time to use it is gone. You'll see the hat again. I'm sure."

"I didn't want to see it," Bruce said.

"Oh?"

"I hid it away on the top shelf, Oliver. Where I couldn't see it."

"It brought back memories that were too painful?"

"Yes."

Oliver turned to him.

"Bruce," he said gently, his eyes soft and understanding. "What really happened that night?"

Bruce stared at him.

"But . . ."

"I know that you tried to tell me. And I stopped you each time that you did. But now I feel up to it. Tell me, Bruce."

Bruce looked away from him and out to the passing trees and the night that was beyond them.

"I caused the accident that killed Raymond. I was drunk."

Oliver's hand tightened over the wheel and then it hung loose again.

"How did you cause it?"

Bruce didn't speak.

"How, Bruce?"

"I . . . I pulled the hat off Raymond's head. The car went into the tree."

Bruce bowed his head and wept silently. Oliver put his hand on Bruce's shoulder and patted it tenderly.

"It's over, Bruce," he said. "It's over."

But when he turned back to the road, there was a serene look in his eyes.

"It will never be over," Bruce said.

They rode along and soon they passed the Carter farmstead and Oliver slowed the car down as they came to a wooded section that rose dark and amorphous before them. Oliver turned the car onto a dirt road and drove about a hundred yards in and came to a halt. They sat there in the night silence.

"The house is up there through the trees," Oliver said in a low voice.

"I know," Bruce said. "The Bensons used to live there."

"They're long gone," Oliver said.

Oliver turned off the lights of the car.

"Someone's in the house," he said. "We're in luck."

Bruce gazed through the trees and saw a light glimmering.

"Open the glove compartment, Bruce."

Bruce pressed the button and the small door swung open with a sharp click.

"Want the searchlight, Oliver?"

"Yes. And the gun. Take it out."

Bruce turned to him and saw Oliver's face white and taut in the darkness. He thought he could see a faint, cruel smile on Oliver's lips.

"It's one of my father's guns. Good to have along."

"But why a gun, Oliver?"

Oliver's lips thinned and his voice became hard.

"Take it out, Bruce. Do as I say."

Bruce switched on the searchlight and then saw in its gleam the automatic lying on the floor of the compartment. Its muzzle was pointed outward, straight at him, like a dark and menacing eye.

"Do you really think we need it, Oliver?"

A glitter came into Oliver's eyes and it sent a tremor through Bruce. *I can't read you, Oliver. I just can't.*

He heard Oliver's harsh voice.

"Christ, Bruce. Your life's on the line. Take the goddamn gun, will you. And keep it ready."

"All right," Bruce said.

He reached in and took out the gun. It lay cold in his grasp.

"I have one, too," Oliver said.

He held up his long hand and Bruce saw the glint of metal.

"Let's get going," Oliver said quietly.

They moved away from the car and slid through the trees toward the house. It was a low wooden structure of no more than four rooms. It stood there, alone in a small clearing.

Its lone light glimmering.

A slight wind came up and the trees shook and the leaves murmured low and then the wind moved on and the night silence fell over them again. The only sound they could now hear was the distant, occasional passing of a car on the narrow highway. It seemed to come from another world.

They neared the house and Oliver stopped and motioned for Bruce to wait. He crouched and went swiftly up to the lit window. He gradually straightened up to his full height and peered in. He turned and motioned Bruce to come up to him.

"I don't see anybody in there." he whispered.

"Where do you think he is?"

"I don't know. I'm going around to the back. Wait here for me."

Oliver's form melted into the darkness. Bruce flattened himself against the wooden wall and he stood there, cold and trembling, waiting anxiously for Oliver's return.

I'm lost, lost in a nightmare, he said to himself. It started the instant I got into that car with Raymond. As if some giant hand closed in on me and held me tight.

But then he said to himself, I made my own fate. Why fool myself? I made it all on my own.

At that instant he saw again the form of Oliver glide

up to him and saw the white, taut face and heard again the flat voice.

"I'm sure there's nobody in the house. But he's around here somewhere."

"But how do you know it's the . . ."

"His hat's there on the table, Bruce. The white panama hat."

"Oh."

"I'm going in there just to look around. You wait out here. Keep your hand ready on your gun."

And before Bruce could speak, Oliver had run to the front door and put his long hand on the doorknob. He swung the door open and vanished within the house.

Bruce stood there, staring at the closed door. He turned and peered into the woods about him, expecting to see at any moment the gaunt figure of Reverend William Dunn come out from among the trees, his face long and haggard and the cat eyes glowing in the darkness.

I'm alone, he said to himself. So naked and alone.

He turned back to the house and suddenly the light went out and the house became a black form. A thrill of terror swept over him.

He stood there, trembling, waiting for the light to go on again. Or for the door to open and Oliver to appear.

The minutes went by. Slow and interminable.

"Christ," he whispered.

He gripped the gun tight and went slowly to the door. He put his free hand to the cold knob, opened the door, and stepped into the house.

The room was dark and yet he could faintly make out the outlines of the table. There was no white panama hat on the table.

The room was dark and silent and empty.

"Oliver?"

Again he called the name.

"Oliver?"

Suddenly he saw a form rise up in front of him and saw the glint of metal and felt a jarring blow on his head.

His knees buckled and he sank to the floor into a ringing darkness.

29

He slowly opened his eyes and the moonlight was coming through the window and there in the corner of the room he saw a tall figure with a floppy hat and the eyes, deep and sunken, and then the lean face, and he screamed.

"Raymond!"

His scream filled the night and fell away into the vast silence.

"Get up."

As he got to his feet he realized that his two hands were manacled behind his back and that the voice was the voice of Oliver.

"Move to the door."

He saw the gun in Oliver's long hand. The hard, dry glitter in the large eyes. And the truth of it all exploded about him.

"You?"

That was all he said.

"To the door."

Oliver pushed him violently forward and opened the door and the night was there before them.

The endless night.

"Start walking."

"Oliver."

"Start, goddamn you, or I'll put a bullet in your head now."

The face under the floppy hat was small and tight. But it was the eyes that struck terror in Bruce.

They were the eyes of a madman.

"Turn to the back of the house. Go on."

Bruce began to walk and there was a path that led past the house and into the woods. The air was quiet. The trees were tall and still around them. The moon glinted its cold silver over the long and twisted branches.

The branches seemed to be covered with winter snow.

I never left that night, he thought to himself. Never. Dear God, show a little pity. Just a little pity.

And then he said to himself, What right do I have to ask for pity? He set his teeth against the terror and walked straight ahead. Behind him walked Oliver, the muzzle of the gun hard in Bruce's back.

They came to a small clearing and they stopped. There in the center of the clearing was a deep trench, the earth piled on either side of it.

A long-handled shovel lay across the trench.

Oliver stooped and picked up the shovel.

"Your grave," he said and pushed Bruce down into it.

Bruce fell and landed hard on the earth. He felt a sharp pain in his shoulder but he feverishly fought to his feet. He saw the figure of Oliver standing above him, full and gleaming in the stark moonlight.

The face was like a silver mask.

The lips of the mask moved and he heard the words.

"The first was by fire. The second by water. And the third by earth."

A shovelful of earth fell onto Bruce, covering his hair and his eyes.

"Oliver!" he cried out. "For the love of God listen to me!"

Oliver held the shovel poised.

"You talk to me of God? You? You drunken murderer. All of you killed Raymond. All of you. You drunken louts. I knew you did it. I knew from the very beginning. He called me from Carlson's. Called to tell me that you were all drunk and I told him to leave you there and come on home. I told him that. I pleaded with him. I ordered him to come home. But you were his friends. His friends."

Oliver's voice rose to a scream.

"He died because of his friendship for you. And now you talk of God. You killed him. And with that you killed me, too. We were going to spend our lives together. We had such dreams. Such plans. To become great architects. You destroyed the dream. And now you talk of mercy. There is no mercy in this life. There is justice and there is execution."

"You have a gun," Bruce said. "Shoot me and get it over with. At least give me that. At least that."

Oliver shook his head grimly.

"By fire, by water, and by earth. I set the fire that killed Edward Millman. With the murderess, Elaine Ross, it was by water. I saw you in the boat with her. I was on the Point standing there under the trees. I knew she'd come out again. I would wait till eternity for her to come out again. And she did. I got into my boat and forced her in toward shore. I made her dive into the water and swim. Swim for her life."

"Let me alone!" Bruce suddenly shouted. "I don't want to hear any more!"

Oliver laughed, a fierce, brittle laughter that pierced the night.

"But you shall. You shall. I made her swim. Swim for her life. And all the time she kept pleading with me to let her back into the boat. But I made her swim. Made her swim to exhaustion. And then she slowly sank under the water and the last thing I saw of her, the last thing I saw, before the water covered everything, was Raymond's exultant face!"

Bruce bowed his head as if Oliver's words were blows.

The earth began falling upon him.

"The Lord punished through the elements, Bruce. From the beginning of time. He still does. The elements of fire and of water and of earth. I am his executioner."

The earth kept coming into the grave, relentlessly. It was up to Bruce's waist.

"No one will ever find you again, Bruce. No one knows you went with me. And if they did, I'll lie and tell them I dropped you off and went on home. You'll disappear from the face of the earth. Forever and ever. So be it. And then my work will be over."

The earth was up to Bruce's neck. And suddenly the terror left him and all that remained was a great pity for Oliver.

"Oliver," he said.

He saw Oliver pause and look down at him.

"Oliver, I'm going to die. I see no hope anymore. I'm sorry for what I did. There's nothing more I can say on that. But I'm making one last plea to you. It's for you, Oliver. For you. Turn back. Get help. You need help badly, Oliver. You've lost your way. Turn back, Oliver."

"No!" Oliver shouted. "There is no turning back. There is only rest when I finish my task. Only then can I rest. Only then."

He picked up the shovel and Bruce closed his eyes and knew that he would never open them again.

At that instant he heard the voice break through the stillness of the night.

"Oliver!"

Bruce opened his eyes and saw the figure of Dan Warner come into the clearing. He held his police revolver in his hand.

Oliver turned slowly and stared at his father.

"Drop the shovel, Oliver. Drop it."

"He killed Raymond," Oliver said in a pleading voice.

"I know. The shovel."

"He and the others. They killed him. Killed your son. Killed my brother. Don't you understand?"

Bruce saw a great haunting sadness come into Dan Warner's eyes.

"I understand, Oliver," he said.

Oliver dropped the shovel.

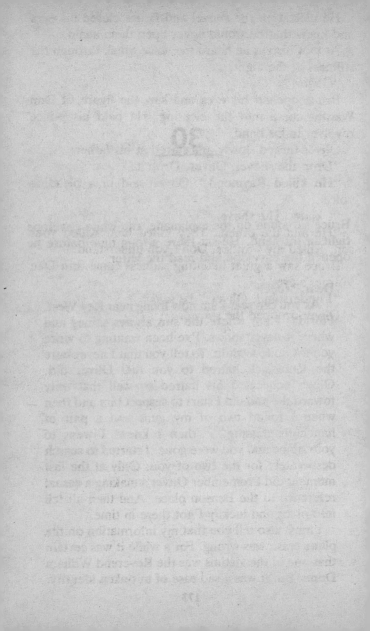

30

Bruce sat alone on the esplanade, the white envelope tight in his hand. He sat there a long time before he opened the envelope and read the letter.

Dear Bruce,

As you can see, I am now living near Key West, Florida. I am where the sun always shines and where it never snows. I've been wanting to write you for quite a while. To tell you that I never bore the same sick hatred to you that Oliver did. Oliver concealed his hatred so well that only toward the end did I start to suspect him and then when I found two of my guns and a pair of handcuffs missing . . . then I knew. I went to your home and you were gone. I started to search desperately for the two of you. Only at the last moment did I remember Oliver's making a casual reference to the Benson place. And then all fell into place and luckily I got there in time.

I must also tell you that my information on the plane crash was wrong. For a while it was certain that one of the victims was the Reverend William Dunn. But it was a sad case of mistaken identity.

Dunn, as you maintained, was very much alive. I checked him out quite thoroughly and found him guiltless. He was a disturbed man who believed deeply and felt he had a mission in life to warn sinners, particularly the young sinners. But he was alive and innocent and I told Oliver that. I talked to him about the Reverend Dunn. But he never told you that. I also feel, Bruce, that I was unnecessarily harsh and abrupt with you at times. Even cruel.

Bruce, I am writing you to tell you that I wish you well. That you are not to go through life carrying a burden of guilt with you. For you are not guilty. There is really, when all is said and done, only one person in this life who has the right to judge you. I believe that I, who have lost two sons, am that person.

Sincerely yours,
Dan Warner

Bruce sat on the bench looking out over the water, the letter tight in his hand. He sat there a long, long time. He became aware of someone sitting next to him. He turned. It was his father.

"Good news, Bruce?" his father asked in a tentative voice.

Bruce gazed at him with clear eyes.

"Yes," he finally said.

And then he said again, "Yes."

JAY BENNETT has won in two successive years, The Mystery Writers of America's Award for the "best juvenile mystery." The author of many suspense novels for young adults, Mr. Bennett has also written successful adult novels, stage plays, and radio and television scripts.

Mr. Bennett's professed aim in his young adult novels (that have sold over a million and a half copies) is "to write honest books that speak about violent times . . . but throughout the books, and in every word I write, there is a cry against violence."

Avon Flare Presents Powerful Novels from Award-winning Authors

Joyce Carol Thomas

Bright Shadow   84509-1/$4.50 US/$6.50 Can
Marked by Fire   79327-X/$4.50 US/$6.50 Can

Alice Childress

A Hero Ain't Nothing But a Sandwich
                           00312-2/$4.50 US/$5.99 Can
Rainbow Jordan   58974-5/$4.50 US/$5.99 Can

Virginia Hamilton

Sweet Whispers, Brother Rush
                           65193-9/$4.99 US/$6.50 Can

Theodore Taylor

The Cay   01003-8/$4.50 US/$5.99 Can
Sniper   71193-1/$4.50 US/$5.99 Can
The Weirdo   72017-5/$4.50 US/$5.99 Can
Timothy of the Cay   72119-8/$4.50 US/$5.99 Can